Samuel French Acting Edition

I0591841

Looking

A Comedy

by Norm Foster

SAMUELFRENCH.COM   SAMUELFRENCH.CO.UK

FOR PRODUCTION ENQUIRIES

UNITED STATES AND CANADA
Info@SamuelFrench.com
1-866-598-8449

UNITED KINGDOM AND EUROPE
Plays@SamuelFrench.co.uk
020-7255-4302

Each title is subject to availability from Samuel French, depending upon country of performance. Please be aware that *LOOKING* may not be licensed by Samuel French in your territory. Professional and amateur producers should contact the nearest Samuel French office or licensing partner to verify availability.

MUSIC USE NOTE

IMPORTANT BILLING AND CREDIT REQUIREMENTS

LOOKING was first produced at the Victoria Playhouse in Petrolia, Ontario, in June of 2005. The set and costumes were designed by Ivan Brozic. The production was directed by Brian McKay with the following cast:

ANDY...Ralph Small
MATT...Ed Sahely
VAL..Melodee Finlay
NINA..Mary Long

CHARACTERS
(All of the characters are in their mid-forties to early fifties)

Andy

Matt

Val

Nina

TIME
The present

PLACE
A tennis club

ACT I

(Lights up to reveal two middle-aged men, ANDY and MATT, in tennis clothes and holding tennis racquets. ANDY is doing some stretches, warming up for a game.)

ANDY. I'm running out of ideas, Matt. I mean, if you go to a bar to look for women, then everybody there knows you're looking. You feel conspicuous.

MATT. So, you want to find a place where nobody expects you to be looking for women.

ANDY. ight.

MATT. Funeral home.

ANDY. What?

MATT. A funeral home. Crash a funeral and then tag along for the wake.

ANDY. Are you out of your mind?

MATT. No, I'm serious. There's always women around because they want to comfort the bereaved. They're dressed in black which is a slimming tone. And there's food.

ANDY. I'm not crashing a stranger's funeral. How insensitive do you think I am? I mean, if somebody dies that I know then great, I'm there. *(He stretches some more and sings the first line of a well known 1970's pop song. He doesn't know the second line so he just sings dada- dee to the song's tune.)*

MATT. How about a cruise?

7

LOOKING

ANDY. You mean on a ship?

MATT. No, in a Volkswagen. Yes, on a ship. They have cruises for singles. And I hear they're just like these huge floating orgies. People are falling overboard having sex.

ANDY. Is that all you think I want? Sex?

MATT. You mean it's not?

ANDY. I want a relationship with a woman. I want something with a solid foundation. I'm not just looking for sex. I can get sex anytime I want it.

MATT. Really?

ANDY. No. God, at my age, are you kidding? It's a young man's world out there, Matt. I feel like it's passing me by. I mean, I look in the mirror these days and I see my father. It's frightening.

MATT. Why? Was he an ugly man?

ANDY. No, he was quite handsome in fact. That's not the point. The point is, I'm aging and I don't like it. Aren't you going to warm up?

MATT. No, I might pull something. You know, Andy, some of these cruises stop at topless beaches.

ANDY. Would you forget the cruises? I'm not going on a cruise. Besides, they cost too much.

MATT. Yeah, but they're all-inclusive.

ANDY. All-inclusive. There's the biggest rip-off since earth shoes. I couldn't drink enough liquor in a month to justify a week of all-inclusive.

MATT. They have food too.

ANDY. It still costs too much.

MATT. My God, you're cheap.

ANDY. I'm careful with my money. Careful. There's a big difference. Topless beaches. Why would you want to go to a topless beach?

MATT. Why? Why do you think?

LOOKING

ANDY. To see topless women? No, a man should have to work to see a woman's breasts. It should be a reward. They shouldn't just be thrust out there indiscriminately. You shouldn't be able to view them like you were strolling through a cabbage patch. *(He sings the first line of another well known 1970's pop song. He doesn't know the second line so he just sings dada-dee to the song's tune.)* Maybe I should put an ad in the personals.

MATT. What?

ANDY. The personals. The newspaper.

MATT. Andy, you're not serious.

ANDY. What's wrong with that?

MATT. The personal ads?

ANDY. Why not?

MATT. I thought you said you didn't want people to know you're looking.

ANDY. This is different. It's anonymous. There's no name attached. You put the ad in, sign your initials and the woman calls you.

MATT. And what would you say in this ad?

ANDY. Uh, well, single white male, late forties..

MATT. Early fifties.

ANDY. Successful businessman.

MATT. Struggling financially.

ANDY. Plays tennis.

MATT. Sucks at tennis.

ANDY. Looking for a woman to share my life with.

MATT. Your life?

ANDY. Some time?

MATT. A night.

ANDY. No, that's not what I'm looking for. I told you I want more than that.

MATT. Well, not me. A relationship is too much work. I think

LOOKING

I'll just keep doing what I'm doing. Having lots of casual sex with women I barely know.

ANDY. When was the last time you had it?

MATT. Bout' a year.

ANDY. Was it good?

MATT. It was too good.

ANDY. Too good? How can it be too good?

MATT. Well, it wasn't normal. I thought 'skills like this can only come from years of professional training'. It was very unsettling...... I should call her.

(ANDY sings the first line of a well known up tempo 1970's rock song. He doesn't know the second line so he just sings dada-dee to the song's tune.)

MATT. You know that's a very annoying habit you have there.

ANDY. What is?

MATT. You sing the first line of a song and you da da dee the rest of it.

ANDY. Well, I only know the first line.

MATT. It's *(He says the name of the song and then recites the first two lines.)*

ANDY. Really? I never knew that.

MATT. How can you not know that? It's a classic.

ANDY. Oh yeah, that's easy for you to say. You're a disc jockey.

MATT. I'm not a disc jockey. I'm a broadcaster.

ANDY. What's the difference?

MATT. A disc jockey just plays music. A broadcaster has a personality. He communicates ideas.

ANDY. Oh. *(He sings the first line of the same rock song again.)*

MATT. Have you got balls?

ANDY. *(He sings the next line with more balls.)*

LOOKING

MATT. No, tennis balls. Have you got tennis balls?

ANDY. Oh. No, I didn't bring any.

MATT. Well, neither did I.

ANDY. So, what are we gonna do?

MATT. Well, we'll have to go in and buy some, won't we?

ANDY. How much are they?

MATT. They're five dol.... my God.

ANDY. What?

MATT. I just realized something. In all the years we've been playing tennis, you've never bought tennis balls.

ANDY. Well, you've always got some.

MATT. I can't believe this. You've never bought a can of tennis balls.

ANDY. So what?

MATT. In six years of tennis, not one can of balls. That is unbelievable.

ANDY. All right, so I'll buy this one.

MATT. No, no. No, a record like that should not be broken. It's like DiMaggio's hitting streak. It should go on forever.

ANDY. Matt, I'll buy the balls.

MATT. No, I don't want you to. I want this record to stand. I want to be able to tell people that I play tennis with the cheapest son of a bitch who ever lived.

ANDY. Fine. Buy them then.

(MATT EXITS. ANDY sings the first line of the same rock song and sings dada-dee to the tune of the second line. ANDY EXITS. Lights up to reveal two middle-aged women, VAL and NINA, in workout clothes at a gym. VAL is working out with some hand weights. NINA is sitting, reading a newspaper.)

VAL. I'm not really looking. I mean, looking makes it sound

LOOKING

like I'm on the prowl or something. I would just like to find a nice guy that I can spend some time with.

NINA. Val, to find something you have to look for it. And if you're looking, you're looking.

VAL. But, I don't want to do that. True romance should just happen, don't you think? It should be kismet.

NINA. So, you think a nice guy should just fall into your lap.

VAL. Well, I'd like to get to know him a bit first.

NINA. Well, I'm sorry, but I don't believe in kismet. I guess I'm jaded. If you're going to find somebody, you have to do the leg work. Go to bars, singles clubs.

VAL. Oh, God, Nina, I wouldn't do that. I mean, what kind of guys are you going to meet in bars? And singles clubs? Please.

NINA. Well, what about at work?

VAL. I work in a hospital. Who am I going to meet in a hospital? The diseased and disfigured.

NINA. What about doctors?

VAL. That's who I was talking about.

NINA. All right, how about this? The personal ads.

VAL. Oh, come on.

NINA. What's wrong with that?

VAL. Would you answer a personal ad?

NINA. Not on your life.

VAL. But, you think I should.

NINA. Well, you're more desperate than I am.

VAL. I'm not desperate. I'm just...I'm the kind of woman who likes to be in a relationship, that's all. I like the benefits of a relationship.

NINA. Which are?

VAL. Having someone to call just to say hi to. Someone who will listen to you when you've got nothing important to say. Someone you can reach out and touch in bed every night. And someone

LOOKING

who, when you have to get up to pee, will turn the radio on so they can't hear you.

NINA. But, if you're not in a relationship, and you get up to pee, there's no one there to hear you anyway.

VAL. What is that, philosophy? Because I hate philosophy.

NINA. Well, relationships are where you and I differ. Personally, I've never found the need for a long term relationship.

VAL. What about sex?

NINA. What about it?

VAL. Don't you feel the need for that?

NINA. Who says I've been without it?

VAL. What?

NINA. Nothing.

VAL. Nina?

NINA. What?

VAL. What are you saying?

NINA. Nothing.

VAL. Have you done it recently?

NINA. It depends on what you call recently.

VAL. In the last month?

NINA. Done it.

VAL. You're kidding. With who?

NINA. Just a guy.

VAL. What do you mean just a guy? Is it serious? Well, it must be serious. You're sleeping with him.

NINA. Oh, come on, Val. Who are you, Heidi? You don't have to be in a relationship to have sex you know. You can meet a guy you like and it just happens.

VAL. And then what?

NINA. And then you lose interest or he loses interest or you find out he's married.

VAL. He was married!!?

LOOKING

NINA. Well, I didn't know.

VAL. Nina Gregorian! I am shocked.

NINA. I didn't know!

VAL. So, how was it?

NINA. Oooh, I was tossin' and turnin' all night.

VAL. Are you a lights out girl or a lights on?

NINA. Oh, God, lights out. I mean, you never know what you're going to see when the clothes come off, right? No, I don't like being surprised. What about you? Lights on or off.

VAL. I forget. It's been so long. I mean, ever since I divorced that lying, skirt-chasing, Pink Floyd-loving Peter, I haven't done it once.

NINA. Yeah, what is it with middle-aged men and Pink Floyd? God, get over it already. What did you say?

VAL. When?

NINA. Just now. Did you say you haven't done it once since your divorce?

VAL. Not once.

NINA. But you've been divorced for six years.

VAL. Tell me about it. Two more celibate years and I regain my virgin status.

NINA. Six years, huh?

(She stares at VAL.)

VAL. Yep.

NINA. Wow.

VAL. What's wrong?

NINA. Nothing.

VAL. No, you're looking at me like I'm the Elephant Man.

NINA. Well, Val, I mean six years. God. Maybe after that long, I would be combing the personal ads.

LOOKING

VAL. What's the longest you've gone without it?

NINA. Well, I don't know exactly, but I know it wasn't measured in years.

VAL. Are you going to work out at all?

NINA. Work out? I don't come here to work out. I come because I look good in the outfit. Why the hell would I want to work out?

VAL. To get in shape?

NINA. What do I have to get in shape for?

VAL. You're a cop. What if you have to chase somebody?

NINA. Val, that's what I have a gun for.

VAL. Well, working out is good for you. And at our age we should be thinking about our health.

NINA. At our age. I hate it when people throw age in your face. At your age you should be thinking about university. At your age you should be thinking about marriage. At your age you should be at your sexual peak.

VAL. What is the sexual peak for women anyway?

NINA. Thirty-five to forty.

VAL. Great. I missed it. I could have shown somebody a good time too.

NINA. Six years, huh? Wow.

VAL. So, what do these personal ads say anyway?

NINA. What, you're interested now?

VAL. No, I'm not interested. I'm just curious.

NINA. Well, let's see here. 'Single white male. Forties. Looking to be smothered in love'. Smothered, huh? Apparently he's looking for a much larger woman than yourself. Uh..'Single white male. Fifty-five. Looking for a woman around thirty.' Jerk. 'Single white male. Late forties. Successful businessman. Plays tennis.' Boring.

VAL. What's wrong with that?

NINA. Plays tennis? That's two doors down from lawn bowling. All right, I'm gonna hit the showers.

(NINA sets the newspaper down and EXITS. VAL picks up the paper and looks at it. Lights down on VAL. Lights up on a table and four chairs. We are now at The Private Dick, a downtown pub. MATT and ANDY are seated at the table. ANDY is wearing a boutonniere.)

ANDY. Waitress? Excuse me?!.... Did you see that? She's ignoring me. And you know why?

MATT. Why?

ANDY. Because I'm not twenty-five and cute. Huh? Look at that. Look. She went straight for the hunk in the white t-shirt.

MATT. Ooh, he is a hunk.

ANDY. I used to look like that.

MATT. Really?

ANDY. Well, I had a white t-shirt once. So, listen, I've been thinking about what I can do to make a good impression on this woman. You know, this being the first date and all? So, what do you think of this? I start off by saying 'You know, I read something the other day that touched me very deeply.' And then I lay this on her. 'O that 'twere possible, after long grief and pain, to find the arms of my true love round me once again.'

MATT. ..... What the hell was that?

ANDY. What?

MATT. What was that?

ANDY. It's poetry.

MATT. Poetry? That's how you plan to impress a blind date? With poetry?

ANDY. It's good.

MATT. It's what? It's good?

ANDY. It's good.

LOOKING

MATT. How do you know it's good?

ANDY. It was in a book.

MATT. A book.

ANDY. In the library.

MATT. Oh, well if it was in the library then say no more.

ANDY. But, it's romantic. You don't think it will impress her?

MATT. Andy, there is no way in the world that today's woman can be impressed by soppy sentimentality. They're too jaded. We all are. Nobody cares about romance anymore. All we care about is sex and power. And believe me, neither one has anything to do with romance. And what the hell were you doing in a library?

ANDY. I was using their washroom. Somebody left the book in the stall.

MATT. Oh.

ANDY. So, you don't think I should use it on her.

MATT. Definitely not. Besides, we're in a pub called The Private Dick. I really don't think this is the kind of place where you lay poetry on a woman. Unless it rhymes with Nantucket. And why did you tell them to meet us here in the first place?

ANDY. Well, it's close to the arena. I figured we'd have a couple of drinks here to break the ice and then walk over to the concert.

MATT. Concert. A man my age, on a blind date, going to see a band called The Holy Trolls. My God, is this what my life has come to?

ANDY. Well, at least you're out instead of sitting at home like you do every other night.

MATT. I like sitting at home. What's wrong with sitting at home?

ANDY. Your life is in a state of atrophy. That's what's wrong.

MATT. Oh, and The Holy Trolls are going to change that are they?

ANDY. The Trolls are very big right now. Metal rap is huge these days.

LOOKING

MATT. Metal rap, huh? And what's the name of their CD?

ANDY. Yo Kiss My Ass.

MATT. Sweet Mother. So, how holy are these trolls anyway? Are they full blown Catholic trolls or just part-time Presbyterian trolls?

ANDY. Listen, stop complaining. I got these tickets for free and by God I'm going to use them.

MATT. Oh, so that's why we're going. The fact that it's The Holy Trolls has got nothing to do with it.

ANDY. No, that's not true. This band is hot. Man, you are out of the loop, my friend. Way out.

MATT. And I'm glad to be out. Give me Pink Floyd any day. Dark Side Of The Moon. Now, there was an album.

ANDY. Look, by taking these women to see the Trolls, we're showing them that we haven't let time pass us by. That even at our age, we're still on the cutting edge of life.

MATT. I don't want to be on the cutting edge of life. I want to be on the smooth middle part where I can't hurt myself.

ANDY. Well, that's the difference between you and me, Matt. I want to experience life at its most raw. I want to cast off the shackles that bind us to the humdrum of this workaday society. I want to burst the boredom like a two cent balloon and be like our primitive ancestors who explored new horizons armed with nothing more than a sharpened stick. Oops.

(He reaches down to his belt.)

MATT. What's the matter?

ANDY. My pager just went off. *(He looks at the pager.)* I have to call the office.

(He takes out his cell phone.)

LOOKING

MATT. *(Pointing to the phone.)* Don't put your eye out with that sharpened stick.

ANDY. *(To the phone.)* Karen? It's Andy. You paged me?..... Yeah. ..... They canceled the order? Why?......They're going with who?.... Karen?..... Hello?..... Karen... *(To MATT.)* Stupid damned cell phone. It's always breaking up on me. I've lost close to fifteen thousand dollars in sales because of this piece of crap.

MATT. Well, why don't you get a new one?

ANDY. Yeah, right. You know how much these things cost? *(Looking around the bar.)* Where the hell are they? I asked her to meet us at 6:30. And where's that waitress? Man I could use a drink.

MATT. I should have said no, you know? When you asked me to come, I should have just said no.

ANDY. You had to come. She said she wanted to bring a girlfriend along because she was nervous about meeting a guy through the personal ads. You're here to keep the girlfriend occupied. I don't want my attentions divided. I need to focus.

MATT. But, the girlfriend knows that I'm just along because she's along, right?

ANDY. Yes.

MATT. I mean, I don't want her to think that I'm the kind of loser who has to meet women through the personal ads. Not that everybody who uses the personal ads is a loser.

ANDY. Hey, I'm not proud of having to get a date this way, but I'll be damned if I'm going to try and pick up a woman in a bar. I mean, what kind of woman would let someone like me do that? Certainly not the kind I want to go out with.

MATT. Yeah, I'm sure you find a much better class of women on the back page of the Sun.

ANDY. And don't forget. I want you to talk me up to her.

MATT. I know.

LOOKING

ANDY. Talk me up good, all right? Make me look very appealing to her.

MATT. I'll lie through my teeth. So, what's this friend of hers like?

ANDY. Val says she's got a great personality.

MATT. Oh, wonderful.

ANDY. What?

MATT. A great personality? That means she's unattractive.

ANDY. Oh, it does not.

MATT. Look, if the best thing you can say about someone is that they've got a great personality, then that person cannot be physically blessed.

ANDY. Well, what do you care? She's not your date anyway. You two are just along as a buffer.

MATT. And you make sure they know that.

ANDY. Well, I'm not waiting for service any longer. I'm going to the bar to get my own drink. *(He stands.)* Are you coming?

MATT. No, I'm okay. You go ahead.

ANDY. What?

MATT. You go ahead. I'll wait here.

ANDY. Oh, you'd like that wouldn't you?

MATT. What?

ANDY. You'd like me to go off and leave you here to meet the women so you can make the good first impression.

MATT. What are you talking about?

ANDY. You know what I'm talking about. I leave, they show up, and you look like the good guy because you waited here for them while I was more worried about getting myself a drink.

MATT. But, you are more worried about getting yourself a drink.

ANDY. And you're worried about making a good impression.

MATT. I don't even want to be here!

ANDY. Would you just come on please?

MATT. All right. God. *(The men start to leave then MATT notices something.)* Oh, wait.

ANDY. What?

MATT. Two women just came in. Is that them?

ANDY. No. That's not them.

MATT. How do you know?

ANDY. Because I asked her to be carrying a red rose and I said she'd know me by my boutonniere.

MATT. Oh.

(ANDY and MATT EXIT. NINA and VAL ENTER.)

NINA. Are you sure this is the right place?

VAL. I think so.

NINA. It doesn't seem like the kind of place you'd bring a woman on the first date.

VAL. Well, I'm pretty sure he said The Private Dick. I mean, his phone was breaking up quite a bit but I think I heard him right. He said we'd have a drink here and then we'd walk down the street to see Holly Cole.

NINA. That's the only reason I agreed to come tonight. I hope you know that. I mean, I haven't been on a blind date in my life. I wouldn't dream of going on a blind date, but when you said we were going to see Holly Cole, well, I love Holly Cole. So, who's this friend he's bringing along?

VAL. His name is Matt. That's all I know. Andy said he's very nice.

NINA. Very nice. There's the kiss of death. Very nice usually means bald. Bald and eager to impress. I should have said no. When you asked me to come I just should have said no.

VAL. Nina, you had to come. He said he wanted to make it a double date so his friend could come along. I guess his friend doesn't get out much.

NINA. Oh, great. I got dressed up for a bald hermit.

VAL. Oh, jeez, I almost forgot.

(She reaches into her purse and pulls out a red clown nose and puts it on her nose.)

NINA. What are you doing?

VAL. On the phone he asked me to be wearing a red nose.

NINA. What?

VAL. Yeah. And he said I would know him by his big ears.

NINA. Who is this guy, P.T. Barnum? Val, look at yourself. Look what you're doing? First you answer a personal ad and now you're standing in the middle of a bar wearing a clown nose.

VAL. Don't start with me, Nina. I'm divorced, I'm insecure, and I don't catch a man's eye the way I used to.

NINA. Well, you're catchin' a few right now I'll tell ya'.

VAL. Look, I don't like the idea of a blind date any more than you do. But, I'll be damned if I'm going to sit at home on another Friday night picking popcorn off of my housecoat. I mean, I have no social life whatsoever. I work, and I go home. I work and I go home. I'm sick of it. My God, aren't you sick of it too?

NINA. To tell you the truth, I've gotten used to it.

VAL. Gotten used to it, or given up?

NINA. Hey, don't start questioning my life, Bozo. I'm very happy with my life. I've got a profession I like, and I'm not burdened by the distractions of a relationship. I don't need a man. Not for longer than an hour anyway.

VAL. I don't need a man either. I just want to know that if there ever comes a time when I want one, that I'll still be able to get one. I want to know that I still have the necessary social graces. That I can still be desirable when I want to be.

NINA. Desirable to who? The Shriners?

(MATT and ANDY ENTER with drinks.)

MATT. Hey, Andy. Check this out.
ANDY. What?
MATT. The woman with the clown nose.
ANDY. Probably just had a nose job and it didn't take.

(MATT and ANDY sit.)

VAL. Let's sit down.
NINA. Why?
VAL. Well, I feel very conspicuous. People are staring at us. I mean, two women standing alone in a bar, it draws attention.
NINA. Yeah, I'm sure that's what's doing it.
VAL. Here, we'll sit here.
NINA. No, there's two guys sitting there. If we sit with them they'll think we're coming onto them.
VAL. Oh, they will not.
NINA. They will so. They take it as a signal. A green light.
VAL. Well, there's no other place to sit. Come on.
NINA. Val, no.
VAL. Oh, come on.
NINA. Val...
VAL. *(To MATT and ANDY.)* Hi.
MATT.
ANDY. tog. Hello.
VAL. Are these two seats taken?
ANDY. Well, we're expecting someone actually.
VAL. Oh.
ANDY. Sorry.

LOOKING

MATT. Well, they can sit until the others get here, can't they?

ANDY. But, they'll be here any minute.

MATT. Then they can sit for a minute. *(To VAL.)* You can sit until they get here if you like.

NINA. No, that's okay.

VAL. Thank you. We will.

(VAL and NINA sit.)

ANDY. But, as soon as they get here, you know...

VAL. Oh, sure, we'll buzz right off.

(There is a long pause as the women look around nonchalantly and MATT stares at VAL's nose. ANDY sings the first line of another well known 1970's pop song. He doesn't know the second line so he just sings dada- dee to the song's tune.)

MATT. *(To the women.)* Crowded here tonight.

VAL. Yes. Very.

MATT. Of course it is Friday.

VAL. Yes.

MATT. *(To VAL.)* I'm sorry. I have to ask.

NINA. Excuse me? If you're going to hit on us, forget about it. We don't want to be harassed, okay?

MATT. No, I wasn't going to hit on you. I was just going to ask about your friend's nose.

VAL. Oh, the nose. Well, I can explain that. You see, we're on a blind date.

MATT. Oh. How's it going so far?

VAL. No, not us. We're meeting our dates here, and he asked me to be wearing a red nose.

MATT. Oh. Well, I knew there had to be a logical explanation.

LOOKING

ANDY. You're on a blind date?

VAL. Yes.

NINA. Well, I'm not.

ANDY. So are we.

MATT. He is. I'm not.

ANDY. We're meeting two women here.

MATT. One woman. I'm not involved in this.

VAL. Well, that's a coincidence, huh? I mean, what are the chances that four couples would have arranged to show up at the same bar at the same time for blind dates?

ANDY. Pretty slim.

VAL. Boy, I'll say.

ANDY. So, are you nervous?

VAL. About the date? Yeah. A little bit.

ANDY. Yeah, me too. I mean, who knows what we're going to wind up with, right?

VAL. Exactly. Who knows what kind of misfits are out there making blind dates?

ANDY. Mine could be some bitter divorcee who'll spend the whole night complaining about her ex-husband.

VAL. Mine could be somebody like my ex-husband.

NINA. *(To VAL.)* Uh, Sweetie? *(NINA takes the clown nose off of VAL's nose.)* What are the chances that four couples would have arranged to show up at the same bar at the same time for blind dates?

VAL. I know. That's what I said. What are the odds? *(She thinks for a second.)* Oh, my God. Andy?

ANDY. Val?

VAL. Oh, my God.

ANDY. I don't believe it. Hi.

VAL. Hi.

ANDY. Oh, this is my friend, Matt.

VAL. Hi.

LOOKING

MATT. Hi.

VAL. And this is my friend Nina.

NINA. Hi.

MATT. Hi.

ANDY. Hi.

VAL. Well, what do you know about that?

ANDY. What do you know indeed?

VAL. So.

ANDY. So.

MATT. So.

(Beat as the other three turn to NINA.)

NINA. So.

ANDY. Well, isn't this something?

VAL. *(To ANDY.)* You know, your ears aren't so big.

ANDY. Thank you.

VAL. Oh, I love your boutonniere.

ANDY. Thank you again. So, would you like a drink? I'll go to the bar and get you one. The service is really slow here tonight.

VAL. Oh, all right. Thank you. I'll have a gin and tonic.

ANDY. Okay. Tina?

NINA. Nina.

ANDY. Sorry. What can I get you?

NINA. I'll have a keg of beer.

VAL. Nina.

NINA. Just a beer please.

ANDY. All right. One gin and tonic and one beer. Lite beer?

NINA. *(Looks down at her body and then back to ANDY.)* Why?

ANDY. No reason. I was just...

NINA. Regular beer, thanks.

ANDY. Right. I'll be right back. Oh, and don't listen to a word this guy has to say about me while I'm gone. It's a pack of lies. All of it.

(ANDY gives MATT an encouraging nudge on the shoulder and EXITS. There is an awkward pause.)

MATT. .....So, do you like the Dick?
NINA. I'm sorry?
MATT. The pub. The Private Dick. How do you like it?
NINA. Oh. It's fine. I.. uh.. I like The Dick just fine.
MATT. .....Do you live around here?
NINA. No.
MATT. ....Well, where do you live?
NINA. Across town.
MATT. Oh.....That's a nice area. And you live there too, Val?
VAL. Hmm-hmm.
MATT. So, you live in the same neighbourhood? The two of you?
VAL. Uh-huh.
MATT. Good......So, what do you two do? Are you mimes or...
VAL. Well, I'm an OR nurse at the hospital, and Nina's a police officer.
MATT. *(To NINA.)* Really?
NINA. Yes.
MATT. A police officer, huh?
NINA. Yeah.
MATT. Wow.
VAL. And I'm an OR nurse.
MATT. *(To NINA.)* So, you actually go out on patrol do you?
NINA. That's what I do.
MATT. Hmm.
NINA. Something wrong?

LOOKING

MATT. No. I think it's great that you can do that.

NINA. At my age you mean?

MATT. No, at any age. Even yours. I mean, you know, not even yours, but..no I'm impressed.

NINA. Well, thank you.

MATT. Yes, very impressed.

VAL. And what do you do, Matt?

MATT. I'm in radio.

VAL. Oh?

MATT. Yeah, I host the morning show on Cool Jazz.

NINA. Cool Jazz?

MATT. Yeah.

NINA. I listen to that station.

MATT. Well, that's where I work.

NINA. And you host the morning show?

MATT. Yeah.

NINA. But Matt Kennedy hosts the morning show.

MATT. Right. That's me. Matt Kennedy.

NINA. Get the hell out of here.

MATT. No, really.

NINA. Well, what do you know about that? I listen to you all the time. I wake up to you.

MATT. Well, give me a nudge next time so I'll know you're there.

VAL. So, you're a disc jockey, are you?

MATT. Broadcaster, yes.

VAL. Oh. I'm an OR nurse.

NINA. So, you're Matt Kennedy, huh?

MATT. Yep. And you're a cop.

NINA. Yep.

MATT. So, have you ever shot anybody?

NINA. Hell, yeah.

MATT. No kidding?

NINA. Oh yeah. You remember that bank hold-up two years ago where one of the robbers was killed and another was wounded?

MATT. Yeah! That was you? You killed a bank robber?

NINA. No, I got the wounded guy.

MATT. Oh.

NINA. But, I was trying to kill him.

MATT. Wow.

VAL. Yes, and oddly enough, the man she wounded was brought into my OR. That's how we met.

MATT. Brought into your what?

VAL. My OR. Operating room.

NINA. She's an OR nurse.

MATT. No kidding?

VAL. Yes, I'm sorry. I thought I mentioned that.

(ANDY ENTERS with the drinks and sets them down.)

ANDY. Here we go.

VAL. Oh, just in time. Thank you, Andy.

ANDY. So, was I right? Was Matt here bending your ear about me while I was gone?

VAL. No, not at all.

ANDY. Really?

VAL. No, he didn't mention you once.

ANDY. Well, that's a relief. Thanks Matt.

VAL. No, we were just discussing occupations.

ANDY. Oh, right. Now, you're a nurse. You told me that over the phone.

VAL. Yes.

MATT. And Nina's a police officer.

ANDY. Get out.

LOOKING

MATT. Yep.

ANDY. Really?

NINA. That's right.

ANDY. So, you actually go out and chase criminals down.

NINA. I do indeed.

ANDY. Wow, at your....

NINA. At my what?

ANDY. At your...weight. I mean, you're so petite.

VAL. *(Holding up her glass.)* All right, enough about Nina. Here's to a pleasant evening on the town.

ANDY. You betcha.

(They all toast.)

ANDY. *(To VAL.)* So, it must be really exciting being an ER nurse.

VAL. OR.

ANDY. OR?

VAL. OR.

ANDY. OR.

MATT. E-I-E-I-O.

(NINA laughs.)

ANDY. So, I take it you don't mind the sight of blood.

VAL. Only in a steak.

ANDY. Well, it must be very exciting.

VAL. Oh, it has its moments, that's for sure.

ANDY. Yeah, well, things can get pretty hairy in my line of work too. Pretty hairy.

VAL. You rent out storage sheds, right?

ANDY. Oh, not just storage sheds. No, ma'am. No, we rent out

LOOKING

sheds, lockers, containers. All manner of storage facility. From the smallest to the largest.

NINA. And that gets hairy, does it?

ANDY. Oh yeah.

MATT. Yeah, Andy's always getting people with gunshot wounds coming into to rent Tupperware.

(NINA and MATT laugh.)

ANDY. All right, so it's not a life and death kind of thing. But, it can get pretty...you know, it's a tough business sometimes.

VAL. I'm sure it's very tough. Goods and services is a very competitive field. I know I couldn't do it.

ANDY. Thanks.

VAL. So, how did you two meet?

ANDY. I rented Matt a storage shed after his marriage broke up. He needed a place to store his stuff.

MATT. Yeah, I had so much. A pair of shorts and a night light.

VAL. So, are you both divorced?

ANDY. Uh-huh.

VAL. Kids?

ANDY. Oh, yeah.

MATT. Yep.

ANDY. You want to see pictures?

VAL. Just try and stop me. I've got pictures too.

MATT. Me too.

(ANDY and MATT both take out their wallets and begin showing pictures. VAL takes some pictures out of her purse and she shows them to ANDY and MATT.)

ANDY. Yeah, I never go anywhere without them. This is my

son Greg. He's twenty-four.

VAL. Oh, handsome.

ANDY. Yeah, that kid's broken a few hearts I'll tell ya.

MATT. This is Belinda and Jake. They're both in university.

VAL. Oh, they're beautiful. He's got your eyes.

MATT. That's what they say.

VAL. Here's my Sarah. She's twenty.

ANDY. Oh, she's gorgeous.

MATT. Very pretty.

VAL. Yes, she's not a baby anymore.

ANDY. They grow up fast, don't they?

MATT. Too fast.

VAL. You can say that again.

NINA. *(Raises her glass in the direction of the bar.)* Two more please!!

MATT. Do you have kids, Nina?

VAL. No, Nina's never been married.

ANDY. Really? At your...uh..

NINA. At my what? Weight?

VAL. Nina? *(To ANDY.)* She gets a little defensive when it comes to her marital status.

NINA. No, I don't.

VAL. Yes, you do.

NINA. No, I don't.

MATT. Hey, I can understand why you're not married. I imagine most guys are intimidated by your profession, right? I mean guys have this macho mindset where they have to be the strong ones in the relationship. Where they have to take care of the woman. Protect her. But you're a cop. You protect people every day. And most guys would be uncomfortable in that setting. They would feel inadequate.

NINA. Is that how you'd feel?

LOOKING

MATT. Oh God no. I'd find it exciting.

NINA. Oh?

MATT. So, what do you do for fun? You know, away from the police station.

NINA. Actually, I'm kind of a homebody.

MATT. Really?

NINA. Yes, I prefer sitting at home. You know, reading. Listening to music. Pretty boring, huh?

MATT. No, not at all.

NINA. I like to cook too. My mother told me to say that. She's old school. Oh, that reminds me, Val. I found those meatless meatballs you've been looking for.

VAL. Oh, where?

NINA. Kinsella's Grocery. It's over on Queen.

ANDY. Meatless meatballs? Wouldn't they just be balls?

VAL. ......Well, listen, shouldn't we be going soon? You said the show starts at 7:30.

ANDY. Yeah, I guess we should be thinking of moving along. We'll just finish our drinks and head off.

VAL. You know Nina really likes Holly Cole.

MATT. Really?

NINA. Oh, yes. Very much.

MATT. I like Holly Cole too.

NINA. You do?

MATT. Yeah, I play her a lot on my show.

ANDY. Well, I hope you like The Holy Trolls as much as Holly Cole.

NINA. Who?

ANDY. The Holy Trolls. The group we're going to see tonight.

NINA. The Holy Trolls. Who the hell are The Holy Trolls? I thought we were going to see Holly Cole.

ANDY. No. The Holy Trolls. So, anyway, I guess we'd better

head off.

    VAL. Yes, let's.

(VAL and ANDY stand.)

    NINA. *(To VAL.)* The Holy Trolls?

    VAL. Yes. Exciting, huh?

    NINA. *(To VAL.)* You said Holly Cole.

    VAL. Holly Cole, Holy Trolls, Dead Sea Scrolls. Who gives a shit?

    ANDY. Ready, Matt?

    MATT. Uh...Listen, Nina, would you like to stay for another drink?

    NINA. Another drink?

    ANDY. But, the show's going to start soon.

    MATT. That's okay. We'll catch up to you. Nina? What do you think?

    NINA. Uh...yeah. Okay. *(To VAL.)* We'll catch up to you.

    ANDY. All right. Here's your tickets. *(He hands MATT two tickets.)* We'll see you inside. Ready, Val?

    VAL. All set.

    ANDY. Good. Well, we'll see you two there.

    MATT. Right.

    NINA. Bye.

    VAL. Bye.

(ANDY and VAL EXIT.)

    MATT. I'm glad you stayed.

    NINA. Well, it beats the Holy Trolls.

    MATT. You know I heard something the other day that really, well, I don't know. It touched me deeply.

LOOKING

NINA. Really? What was that?

MATT. Well, let me see if I can remember it now. Uh....O that 'twere possible, after long grief and pain, to find the arms of my true love round me once again.

NINA. Oh, that's beautiful.

(Lights down on MATT & NINA. ANDY and VAL ENTER. ANDY sings the first line of another well known 1960's or 1970's pop song. He doesn't know the second line so he just sings dada-dee to the tune.)

VAL. Well, thanks a lot, Andy. It was nice.

ANDY. You liked it?

VAL. Yes, it was interesting.

ANDY. The band wasn't too loud I hope.

VAL. Oh, no. No, I like it loud. That way I can hear the lyrics. You know, all that stuff about 'Do it to me mama. Gimme some mo'. Do it to me baby. You a stank-ass ho.'

ANDY. Boy, you sure remember lyrics better than I can.

VAL. Well, the good ones just stick with me.

ANDY. I wonder what happened to Matt and Nina.

VAL. Yeah, I wonder.

ANDY. I hate to see those tickets go to waste.

VAL. Were they expensive?

ANDY. I don't know.

VAL. You don't know how much the tickets were?

ANDY. Uh..well, I didn't really pay attention when I bought them. Money doesn't mean that much to me. It's just money, right?

VAL. Yeah. Well, maybe they just decided that the Holy Trolls weren't their cup of tea.

ANDY. Yeah, probably. Matt's not really in the loop as far as music goes.

VAL. But he has his own radio show.

ANDY. Yeah, right. Jazz.

VAL. Well, to tell you the truth, Nina didn't really want to come tonight, so she probably just made up some excuse to go home.

ANDY. Same with Matt. I practically had to drag him out tonight. I only hope that in his haste to get away he didn't leave your friend sitting alone in the bar.

VAL. Although they did seem to connect there just before we left.

ANDY. No, you know what that was? That was Matt being a good friend. He was backing off so you and I could be alone.

VAL. Do you think?

ANDY. Oh, yeah, he probably saw that we were hitting it off and he didn't want him and Nina to get in the way. That's why he asked her to stay for another drink.

VAL. Oh.

ANDY. Yeah, believe me, there was no chemistry between those two at all.

(An upstage door opens and MATT and NINA ENTER. They are kissing. Throughout the next scene they kiss while trying to get each other's coats off. They try to pull their sweaters off. They make their way slowly across the stage towards NINA's bedroom.)

MATT. Oh, God!

NINA. Oh, God!

ANDY. Matt's actually kind of shy.

VAL. Really?

ANDY. Oh, yeah. He gets nervous around women.

MATT. How far is your bedroom?

NINA. Another twenty feet.

MATT. I don't know if I can wait that long.

VAL. Nina's not shy. It just takes her a while to warm up to a person.

NINA. Oh, God, I want you so bad!

VAL. I just hope she didn't make Matt feel uncomfortable.

NINA. I want those clothes off of you now!

MATT. Is this a strip search?

NINA. It is if you want it to be.

ANDY. I just hope Matt didn't say something stupid.

(Lights down on ANDY and VAL.)

MATT. I've never made out with a cop before.

NINA. And I've never made out with a disc jockey.

MATT. Broadcaster.

NINA. Whatever.

MATT. I want you to Mirandize me.

NINA. What?

MATT. Mirandize me. Read me my rights.

NINA. You have the right to remain silent.

MATT. Oh, yes!

NINA. Anything you say may be used against you in a court of law.

MATT. Oh, God, yes!

NINA. You have the right to consult an attorney.

MATT. Attorney, yes!!!

(MATT and NINA EXIT. Lights up on ANDY and VAL.)

ANDY. *(He sings the first line of another well known 1960's or 1970's pop song. He doesn't know the second line so he just sings dada-dee to the song's tune.)* Listen, if you ever find yourself in need of a storage facility of any kind, I can fix you right up. *(He gives VAL his business card.)*

VAL. Oh, well, thank you.

ANDY. Big or small. And I'll only charge you enough to cover my costs, which is next to nothing.

VAL. I appreciate that.

ANDY. We didn't really get to talk too much tonight, did we?

VAL. Well, with the music and all.

ANDY. Yeah, it was kind of tough. Probably wasn't a good idea for a first date.

VAL. No, it was fine. Really.

ANDY. We could talk now. We can go inside and talk for a while if you like.

VAL. Oh, well, I would but my place is a mess.

ANDY. That's okay. I've seen messy places before.

VAL. Well, I'd feel a little embarrassed that's all.

ANDY. Oh, sure. Well, we passed a coffee a shop just up the street. We could go there and talk.

VAL. You know, I would, Andy, but I've got an early shift to-morrow and I really should get to bed.

ANDY. Oh, okay.

VAL. I can't be going into the OR on no sleep.

ANDY. Sure....Well, then.

VAL. Well, then.

ANDY. I had a really good time tonight.

VAL. I'm glad.

ANDY. It was nice.... So, I guess this is goodnight.

VAL. Yeah.

ANDY. I.. uh... well.

(ANDY leans in for a kiss. VAL backs off a bit but does allow him to kiss her.)

VAL. Oh. Uh..yes...

(It is a very awkward kiss.)

ANDY. Can I call you again? For another date I mean?

VAL. Uh..well, sure, but my schedule is always so up in the air. I never know what shift I'm going to be working from one night to the next.

ANDY. They don't post those things?

VAL. Well, yes but sometimes it's at the last minute.

ANDY. Oh.

VAL. And I get called in for a lot of emergencies too, so...

ANDY. Uh-huh.

VAL. And with that smallpox scare that's on right now, we're all on alert. We're like, eeek! So tense. So it makes it tough to actually schedule something definite.

ANDY. Sure. All right. Well, I'll see you sometime then.

VAL. Right.

ANDY. Goodnight.

VAL. Goodnight.

(ANDY begins to leave then stops.)

ANDY. I'm not going to see you again, am I?

(VAL stops but doesn't answer. VAL EXITS. ANDY EXITS. Lights up on MATT. He is sitting doing his radio show.)

MATT. All right, it's coming up to eight thirty-five on Cool Jazz FM 98. I'm Matt Kennedy. Good morning. I was reading this morning where a seventy-one year old grandmother robbed a gas

LOOKING

station in Calgary. Apparently two days earlier she signed up for the meals on getaway wheels program. And speaking of crime, this next one is going out to a very special lady. A woman in uniform. One of the city's finest. And believe me, she is very fine. *(ANDY ENTERS and stands behind MATT. MATT doesn't see him.)* She is soooo fine. She can charm the birds right out of the trees, and light up a summer night like a shooting star sent from heaven above. If you're listening out there, and I know you are, this one's for you. For every beautiful inch of you.

(We hear a song.)

ANDY. Hi Matt.

MATT. Andy!! What are you doing here?

ANDY. Well, I was on my way to the office and thought I'd stop in for a chat.

MATT. But, how did you get in?

ANDY. I walked in. The front door was open.

MATT. But there's supposed to be a security guard down there.

ANDY. What for?

MATT. To provide security.

ANDY. Security from what?

MATT. Well, what if some nut shows up and wants to hijack the airwaves?

ANDY. Yeah, right. Hijack a jazz station. What's he going to do? Put the city to sleep?

MATT. Well, you're not supposed to be in here. This is the control room. Nobody's allowed in here but the on-air staff.

ANDY. Right. So, what was that all about?

MATT. What?

ANDY. That 'shooting star every beautiful inch of you' crap.

MATT. Oh, that was a request some guy phoned in for his wife.

LOOKING

ANDY. You were laying it on kind of thick, weren't you?

MATT. No, I was just..I mean, that's what the guy asked for.

ANDY. Wow. Talk about your soppy sentimentality.

MATT. Yeah.

ANDY. How embarrassing.

MATT. Uh-huh.

ANDY. The guy sounds whipped.

MATT. Yeah, what are you doing here, Andy?

ANDY. Well, I wanted to find out what happened to you last night. You didn't show up at the concert.

MATT. Oh, yeah, well we decided not to go.

ANDY. We?

MATT. The woman and I. What's her name? Nina. Yeah, neither one of us were really up for it, you know?

ANDY. Didn't hit it off, huh?

MATT. Uh, no it's not that. She was nice. She was fine.

ANDY. So how long did she stay at the Dick?

MATT. I'm sorry?

ANDY. The woman. Did she just leave you sitting there by yourself?

MATT. No. No, we left together actually. And how was your date?

ANDY. Good. Good.

MATT. And?

ANDY. And what?

MATT. Well, give me some details.

ANDY. There are no details. We went to the concert, I spilled a drink on her shoes when some out of control fan bumped my arm, some punk metal head called her grandma, the lead singer jumped into the crowd and inadvertently kicked her in the side of the head, somebody threw a smoke bomb and made her eyes water for half an hour, and then I took her home.

LOOKING

MATT. So, it was pretty uneventful.

ANDY. Pretty much.

MATT. So, are you going to see her again?

(ANDY just stares at MATT for a moment.)

ANDY. Very funny.

MATT. What?

ANDY. She hated me.

MATT. Oh, she didn't hate you.

ANDY. She did.

MATT. Andy.

ANDY. She loathed me. I even offered to give her a discount on storage and she didn't bite. That's how much she hated me.

MATT. Well, maybe she's got nothing to store.

ANDY. Oh, she's got something to store all right.

MATT. Well, I think you should give her another shot.

ANDY. No. I've been humbled enough, thank you. Besides, if she goes out with me again her insurance rates are going to sky-rocket.

MATT. Andy, you've got to go out with her again.

ANDY. Why?

MATT. Because I promised Nina you would.

ANDY. What? What does Nina have to do with this?

MATT. All right, look, I asked Nina to go to the Holly Cole concert with me next week and she said that she would feel bad about going out with me again if you and Val didn't go out because it was Val's blind date and if we hit it off and you and Val didn't then it wouldn't be fair to Val.

ANDY. What?

MATT. I don't know. It's a woman thing. Come on, Andy. Ask her out one more time.

LOOKING

ANDY. Wait a minute. I thought you and this Nina didn't hit it off.

MATT. I didn't say that.

ANDY. So, you like her?

MATT. Yeah, she's nice.

ANDY. So, let me get this straight. It was my blind date, but you end up with the woman. Is that fair?

MATT. You begged me to go.

ANDY. Yeah, as a buffer.

MATT. And that's what I did.

ANDY. What?

MATT. Nothing.

ANDY. You buffed her?!

MATT. Andy, please. Just ask her out would you?

ANDY. No, I can't.

MATT. Come on. You'd be doing me a big favour.

ANDY. Matt, she doesn't like me.

MATT. No, you didn't give her a chance. You've got to turn on the charm.

ANDY. Turn on the charm? I had it up to eleven last night.

MATT. Well, take it up a notch.

ANDY. There are no more notches!! I was charming the ass off her! You should have heard me. I did everything but recite that stupid piece of poetry. So, no, I will not ask her out again.

MATT. Well, thank you very much. Thank you very much. After I went with you last night even though I didn't want to? You won't return the favour? Is that what you're saying?

ANDY. .....How much are the tickets?

MATT. They're on me.

ANDY. What'd you get them for free?

MATT. No, I thought I'd actually pay for them.

ANDY. All right, I'll ask her but she's going to say no, I'll tell you that right now.

MATT. It doesn't matter. As long as you ask her. If she says no then you've made the offer and she's turned it down. That'll release Nina from any guilt.

ANDY. What is that, another woman rule?

MATT. I guess.

ANDY. All right, I'll call her tonight.

MATT. Thank you.

ANDY. God. So refresh me. Who the hell is Holly Cole again?

MATT. She's a jazz singer.

ANDY. Oh, well that sweetens the pot.

(ANDY EXITS. We hear the song that was playing previously. Lights up on VAL. She is working out. NINA ENTERS in her street clothes.)

NINA. Hey.

VAL. Hi, Nina.

NINA. I thought I'd find you here.

VAL. *(Looking at her clothes.)* Not gonna workout again huh??

NINA. Hmm? Oh, no. No, I had a good workout last night.

VAL. What?

NINA. You know, at home.

VAL. You work out at home?

NINA. Not as often as I'd like to.

VAL. So, you didn't come to the concert.

NINA. No, we decided to skip it.

VAL. We?

NINA. Yeah, the guy. What's his name? Matt. We weren't really up for it.

VAL. Didn't hit it off, huh?

NINA. No, it wasn't that. He was fine. He was nice.

LOOKING

VAL. So, how long did you stay at the Dick?

NINA. I'm sorry?

VAL. The bar. Isn't that what he called it? The Dick?

NINA. Oh, right. No. Uh..not too long. And what about you? How was your date?

VAL. Oh, it was all right.

NINA. And?

VAL. And what?

NINA. Well, give me some details. Gimme the dirt.

VAL. There is no dirt. We went to the concert and he took me home.

NINA. Oooh, took you home huh? Now you're talkin'. And then what happened?

VAL. I went inside and he went home.

NINA. You went inside?

VAL. Yeah.

NINA. Alone?

VAL. Of course alone. It was our first date. You don't think I'd do something on the first date, do you? What kind of a skank do you think I am?

NINA. Well, skank's a little judgmental.

VAL. He just wasn't my type, that's all.

NINA. Why not?

VAL. He just wasn't.

NINA. Why?

VAL. I don't know. There was no magic. I need magic.

NINA. Wait a minute. I thought you just wanted a guy who would turn the radio on while you peed? Now you want magic?

VAL. No, I mean, he was a nice guy. He tried hard enough but there was nothing he said or did that set off any sparks. Nothing that made me think, 'Wow, this guy is something special.' I need that.

NINA. Well, I think you should give him a second chance.

VAL. No. There's nothing there. And if I went out with him again I'd just be leading him on.

NINA. No, you wouldn't.

VAL. Yes, I would.

NINA. Val, you have to go out with him again.

VAL. Why?

NINA. Because I told Matt you would.

VAL. What? What does Matt have to do with this?

NINA. Well, Matt doesn't think that Andy is very confident around women and he thinks that if this thing with you and him doesn't go beyond one date then Andy's confidence will be totally shattered and he'll spend the rest of his life alone and it'll be all your fault.

VAL. What?

NINA. I know. Weird, huh? It must be a guy thing.

VAL. So, I have to go out with him to boost his confidence?

NINA. One more date. That's all. And then at the end of the date you make up some excuse why you can't see him again. Like you're joining a convent or a women's softball team.

VAL. Nina, I can't do that.

NINA. Please, Val? For me? I promised Matt that you would, and I don't want him to think that I make empty promises.

VAL. Oh, so this is all about you and Matt?

NINA. Yes, it is.

VAL. So, you like this guy a lot, do you?

NINA. I think I do, yeah.

VAL. This guy that you met on my blind date.

NINA. Yeah. Sorry about that.

VAL. You know what I call that?

NINA. Disloyal?

VAL. Kismet.

NINA. Oh. Yeah, I guess maybe it is.

LOOKING

VAL. And you said you didn't believe in that kind of thing.

NINA. So will you do this for me?

VAL. All right, I'll go out with him one more time, but that's it.

NINA. Thank you.

VAL. You understand that, right? One more time.

NINA. I understand. And we're going to see Holly Cole. And when he calls, make sure you sound excited about going, okay? Thanks, Val. See you!

VAL. Uh, Nina?

NINA. What?

VAL. Did you sleep with this guy last night?

NINA. What? Sleep? Certainly not!

(NINA EXITS. Lights down on VAL. MATT ENTERS S.R. with his cell phone. NINA ENTERS S.L. with her phone.)

NINA. Hello?

MATT. Nina?

NINA. Matt?

MATT. Hi.

NINA. Hi.

MATT. *(Sexier.)* Hi.

NINA. *(Sexier.)* Hi.

MATT. Well, I talked to Andy this morning and he's going to call Val tonight and ask her to the concert.

NINA. Oh, good. I just talked to Val. She'll be expecting his call.

MATT. Is she going to say yes?

NINA. Yeah. She said she'd love to go out with him one more time.

MATT. Really?

NINA. Yeah, why?

LOOKING

MATT. Well, Andy said she hated him.

NINA. No, no. She didn't...hate him. She just said there was no magic.

MATT. No what?

NINA. Magic. She wants magic.

MATT. What, you mean like card tricks?

NINA. No. She wants some ridiculous, unattainable, idealistic sign that he's the one for her.

MATT. Oh. Well, I'll pass that along. So, did you hear my dedication to you this morning?

NINA. Yes, I did. It was very nice.

MATT. And I meant every word. It was great last night.

NINA. It was great for me too.

MATT. So, uh..what are you wearing right now?

NINA. *(Looks down at her clothes.)* Right now? Uh...a slinky black camisole and satin French cut underwear.

MATT. *(Slightly disappointed.)* Oh.

NINA. What's wrong?

MATT. Nothing. I was just hoping you might be wearing your uniform.

NINA. Oh. Well, I'll be going out on patrol in about an hour. I'll be wearing it then.

MATT. Oh, good.

NINA. And I'll try and rough somebody up for you today.

MATT. You're going to give me goose bumps.

NINA. Oh, listen, Matt, the next time you see Andy, tell him this. If by chance he and Val happen to spend the night together, and she has to get up to pee, tell him to turn the radio on.

(ANDY sings the first line fo another well known 1960's or 1970's pop song. He doesn't know the second line so he just sings dada-dee to the song's tune. It would help at this point if the second

*line of the song's lyrics actually contained a dada or a dodo or
a ron-ron so that it makes his forgetting the lyrics seem even
more absurd.*
Lights up on VAL. She answers her cell phone.)

VAL. Hello?
ANDY. Hello?
VAL. Hello?
ANDY. Hello? *(Looks at the phone.)* Stupid piece of crap.
VAL. Hello?
ANDY. Hello, Val?
VAL. Yes?
ANDY. Oh, hi. This is Andy.
VAL. Yes, I recognized the phone.
ANDY. So, how are you?
VAL. Fine.
ANDY. Did I catch you at a bad time?
VAL. No, not at all.
ANDY. Oh, good. I thought with all those last minute shifts and
emergencies and stuff that you might be working, and I'd hate to
interrupt you while you're catheterizing somebody.
VAL. No, I'm at home.
ANDY. Oh, good. So, listen, Matt got these tickets to see some
jazz singer I've never heard of and I guess he and your friend are
going and he wants to know if you and I want to tag along so I said
I'd call and see if you wanted to but it's okay if you don't, it doesn't
really matter to me.
VAL. Yes, I'd love to.
ANDY. *(He bangs the phone into his hand.)* Damn this thing.
Hello?
VAL. Hello?
ANDY. Sorry. My phone's on the fritz. It sounded like you said

yes.

    VAL. I did.

    ANDY. What?

    VAL. I said yes.

    ANDY. .....You know who this is, right?

    VAL. Yes.

    ANDY. Andy? From last night?

    VAL. Yes, I know.

    ANDY. How's your head by the way?

    VAL. Better. The bump's gone down.

    ANDY. And your eyes?

    VAL. Cleared right up.

    ANDY. Good. So, you want to go to this concert, huh?

    VAL. Yes. When is it?

    ANDY. I'm not sure.

    VAL. Where is it?

    ANDY. Haven't got a clue.

    VAL. Sounds like you don't know much about it.

    ANDY. Well, I didn't think I'd have to. I thought you would
have hung up by now.

    VAL. Well, I'm saying yes.

    ANDY. Oh. Well, I'll get the details and get back to you.

    VAL. Good. I'm looking forward to it.

    ANDY. You are?

    VAL. Yes. Very much.

    ANDY. .....This is Val the OR nurse, right?

    VAL. Yes.

    ANDY. Okay. I'll see you later then.

    VAL. Bye.

(Lights down on Val.)

LOOKING

ANDY. *(To himself.)* Hmm. Great. I've got a second date. With a schizophrenic.

(ANDY EXITS. Lights up on NINA. She is answering her cell phone.)

NINA. Hello?

(Lights up on VAL with her cell phone.)

VAL. Nina?
NINA. Val?
VAL. He called?
NINA. He did?
VAL. Just now.
NINA. And?

(Lights up on MATT. He answers his cell phone.)

MATT. Hello?

(Lights up on ANDY with his cell phone.)

ANDY. Matt?
MATT. Andy? .
ANDY. I called
MATT. You did?
ANDY. Just now.
MATT. And?
ANDY & VAL. *(Together.)* Ahhhhh, I don't know.
MATT & NINA. *(Together.)* What's wrong?
VAL. This is crazy.
ANDY. I think she's crazy.

LOOKING

MATT & NINA. *(Together.)* Why?

VAL. I felt bad saying yes.

ANDY. She said yes.

MATT & NINA. *(Together.)* No, no, this is good.

ANDY & VAL. *(Together.)* Ya think?

MATT & NINA. *(Together.)* Yeah, yeah, very good.

ANDY & VAL. *(Together.)* Really?

MATT & NINA. *(Together.)* Extremely good.

ANDY & VAL. *(Together.)* Well...

MATT & NINA. *(Together.)* Trust me.

(There is a long beat as ANDY and VAL think.)

ANDY & VAL. *(Together.)* Ahhhhh, I don't know.

MATT & NINA. *(Together.)* It'll be fun!

ANDY & VAL. *(Together.)* Ya think?.

MATT & NINA. *(Together.)* It'll be great!

ANDY & VAL. *(Together.)* I hope.

MATT & NINA. *(Together.)* It'll be terrific!

ANDY & VAL. *(Together.)* If you say so.

MATT & NINA. *(Together.)* I'll see you then. Bye!!

(They all look at their cell phones, then after a beat.)

MATT, NINA, ANDY & VAL. *(Together.)* Ahhhhh shit.

(Lights down. End Act One.)

ACT II

(Time: The night of the Holly Cole concert. Lights up to reveal ANDY and MATT sitting at a table. They are at The Private Dick.)

ANDY. I don't get it. Why would I have to turn the radio on?

MATT. I have no idea. Just do it.

ANDY. Okay, listen, I really think this woman is nuts.

MATT. What?

ANDY. Completely out of her mind. I mean, one minute she hates me, the next minute she'd love to go out with me, and now I have to turn the radio on when she goes to the bathroom. And let's not forget the clown nose.

MATT. Andy, she's fine. I'm just telling you, if you spend the night with her, do the radio thing.

ANDY. Yeah, right. Do you know what the odds are of Val and me spending the night together? About the same as you and I spending the night together. In fact, the way things are going, I've got my eye on you.

MATT. No, listen, I really think you can pull this off. All she wants is some magic.

ANDY. What?

MATT. She wants some magic.

ANDY. What, I'm supposed to saw her in half? What magic?

MATT. *(He takes out a piece of paper.)* No. Look, I've done some research for you. She wants to hear stuff like this. Listen. *(He*

53

reads.) 'A truly happy person is one who can enjoy the scenery while taking a detour.'

ANDY. What the hell is that?

MATT. It's the kind of adage she wants to hear.

ANDY. I thought you said women didn't go for soppy sentimentality anymore.

MATT. Well, maybe I was wrong. What do I know? Here's another one. *(He reads.)* 'Don't cry because it's over. Smile because it happened.'

ANDY. Because what happened?

MATT. Whatever. Whatever happens.

ANDY. But what if nothing happens?

MATT. That's not the point! All right, never mind. Here's one more. *(He reads.)* 'Let no one who loves be called altogether unhappy, for even love unreturned has its rainbow.'

ANDY. What kind of Hallmark crap is this?

MATT. I'm telling you it'll work.

ANDY. Yeah, if I'm hitting on Maya Angelou.

MATT. *(He gives ANDY the paper.)* Look, just keep it all right? And if you get a chance to work it into the conversation, do it.

ANDY. Oh yeah. I think there's a real good chance of that happening. No, my only hope is to get her really drunk. Drunk women seem to find me very appealing. And why did you tell them to meet us at the Dick? This is where the last fiasco started.

MATT. Holly Cole's playing at a club a couple of blocks from here so it was convenient.

ANDY. And they're late again too. What is this? They can't be on time once?

MATT. So, they're ten minutes late. Big deal.

ANDY. Yeah, a woman is ten minutes late, its okay. A man is ten minutes late, we should castrate the thoughtless bastard! *(He calls out to the waitress.)* Waitress?...Excuse me?...Hello? Ah, the poor thing. Must be hearing impaired. Well, I'm going to get a beer. You want a beer?

(ANDY stands.)

MATT. Sure, thanks.

ANDY. ......You want me to pay for it?

MATT. Sure. Great. I'll get the next round.

ANDY. Uh-huh....Because actually, I'm a little short these days.

MATT. Oh, God. Here we go.

ANDY. Now, I'm not being cheap. I just...Well, business hasn't been good and I've got just enough cash to get me through this date.

MATT. You're kidding? It's that bad?

ANDY. It'll pick up. It's just one of those soft periods, that's all. I've gone through them before.

MATT. Gee, I'm sorry to hear that, Andy.

ANDY. Ah, it's nothing.

MATT. Honestly?

ANDY. I'm sorry I mentioned it.

MATT. All right, sure. I'll buy.

(MATT stands.)

ANDY. Thanks.

MATT. You gonna be okay?

ANDY. Oh, please. Another week and it'll be gangbusters again.

MATT. You sure?

ANDY. Absolutely. Listen, could you spot me a twenty so I can buy a round when they get here?

MATT. I thought you said you had enough to get you through the date.

ANDY. Yeah, to get me through the date. What if she wants a

drink too?

(MATT and ANDY EXIT. VAL and NINA ENTER.)

VAL. I hate being late.

NINA. Oh, what's ten minutes?

VAL. Ten minutes is thoughtless. That's what ten minutes is.

NINA. I don't see them anywhere. Do you?

VAL. Uh...yeah, there they are. They're at the bar.

NINA. Oh. *(She waves.)* Hi boys!

VAL. Good, Nina. Nine men just waved at you. Let's sit down.

(They move to the table and sit.)

NINA. Listen, thanks for doing this for me, Val. I really appreciate it.

VAL. Yeah, but it's just this one time don't forget. This is the last date.

NINA. Hey, you never know. He might have that magic this time.

VAL. He might, but I doubt it.

NINA. Val, did you ever think that maybe you're hoping for too much?

VAL. Too much how?

NINA. Well, I mean, how many really good men our age can there be out there?

VAL. What?

NINA. Seriously. Can there be that many?

VAL. What about Matt? You seem to think he's good.

NINA. Well, Matt's one of the few. I mean, think about it. Why would a guy be out there in the first place? Because he's been rejected by other women. And why? Because he lied, cheated, couldn't

LOOKING

hold a job, was insensitive, indifferent, obnoxious, homely or lousy in bed.

VAL. So, these are the kinds of guys who are out there?

NINA. For the most part, yes.

(VAL stands and looks around the bar.)

What are you doing?

VAL. I'm checking out the women. There's gotta someone in this bloody world who's right for me.

NINA. No, I'm not saying there's no one, Val. I'm just saying don't set your sights too high.

VAL. I beg your pardon?

NINA. You heard me. Aim a little lower.

VAL. Aim a little lower?

NINA. Yeah. *(Looks towards the bar.)* What's keeping those guys?

VAL. You know, Nina, I happen to think that I'm a pretty good catch.

NINA. What? .

VAL. No, I'm a very good catch. I'm smart. I have a good sense of humour. I'm well read, well spoken, I've got a good career, and I can look pretty damn sexy with the right outfit and proper lighting. And you know what else? I've got nice hair. Yeah. No split ends, soft to the touch and easy to manage. And with that kind of package you expect me to aim lower? I don't think so, Missy. In fact, if anything, I'm going to aim just as high as I can, because I think I deserve the best. That's right. Somewhere out there is one very nice, very good-looking, very successful man who is going to meet me and say, 'Wow. Why aren't you spoken for yet?' And I'll say, 'Because I haven't found anyone good enough yet and that includes you, Jerk-off, so hit the road.' So, thanks for the advice, Nina, but no, I will not be setting my sights lower anytime soon. In fact, if anything, you should be setting yours a little higher. Like above the waist.

NINA. What's that supposed to mean?

VAL. Well, you have one date with a guy and you're falling into bed with him.

NINA. Who said we fell into bed?

VAL. Nina, please. I'm not an idiot. Ever since last weekend you've had that satisfied look on your face. And believe me, I know that look, because every time I look in the mirror, I don't see it.

NINA. You know, a woman can look satisfied without having sex.

VAL. Yeah, after a good hunk of chocolate maybe.

NINA. So, you think I'm moving too fast.

VAL. I think you dive in without checking to see what's down there. And you're going to get hurt. And then you'll feel awful. I mean, the last guy you were with was married. How did he make you feel? *(Nina smiles.)* Oh, God, there's the satisfied look again.

(ANDY and MATT ENTER with their drinks. ANDY has a small napkin in his hand. He sets his drink down and begins wiping his hands with the napkin.)

MATT. Hey, you made it. Hi.

(MATT gives NINA a kiss on the cheek.)

NINA. Hi.
MATT. It's good to see you.
NINA. It's good to see you too.
ANDY. Hey, Val.
VAL. Hey, Andy.

LOOKING

(VAL looks at ANDY wiping his hands.)

ANDY. Wet knap. I had some peanuts at the bar and I got salt all over my hands. I hate that.

NINA. I'm sorry we're late but Douglas Avenue was all torn up and we had to reroute through the industrial park.

MATT. Really?

NINA. Oh, God, it was a mess.

MATT. Did you hear that, Andy? They had to take a detour.

ANDY. Yeah, that's a shame.

MATT. You know, Andy has this saying about detours, don't you Andy?

ANDY. What?

MATT. That thing you say about detours.

ANDY. What thing?

MATT. Come on. You must have said it to me a hundred times. How does it go again?

ANDY. I don't know what you're talking about.

MATT. No, you remember. You always say, 'A truly happy person is one who can enjoy the scenery while taking a detour.'

ANDY. Oh, that.

VAL. But we went through the industrial park.

MATT. No, that doesn't matter.

VAL. There's not a whole lot of scenery in the industrial park.

MATT. No, it's not about the industrial park. It's philosophical.

VAL. Oh, I hate philosophy.

ANDY. Me too.

MATT. Never mind.

ANDY. So, can I get you ladies a drink? I'm buying.

NINA. Yes, I'll have a beer please.

VAL. Just a Coke for me thanks. I'm the designated driver.

LOOKING

ANDY. Great.

(ANDY and MATT exchange glances. ANDY EXITS.)

MATT. That Andy. That guy. He's a helluva guy. He's got a heart as big as all outdoors. And funny! Please. He has me in stitches constantly. Great sense of humour. Yeah, he's got quite the personality. And he's a giver. Very generous man. You know, with friends, charities.

(MATT nods at NINA encouraging her to join in.)

NINA. He seems to have good hygiene too.

MATT. Oh, the best! The best. He's always washing himself. He's very conscientious where that's concerned.

VAL. Really?

MATT. Extremely. And thorough. He doesn't miss a spot.

VAL. How is he in bed?

MATT. Again very thorough. Yeah, from what I understand he satisfies from top to bottom.

VAL. All right, Matt, you can stop now.

MATT. Stop what?

VAL. You're his friend, and I know what you're doing, but you don't have to sell me on Andy.

MATT. I don't.

VAL. No.

MATT. So you like him then?

VAL. Sure, I like him. I didn't say I didn't like him.

NINA. But that's all she does.

MATT. What?

NINA. She likes him and that's it.

MATT. That's it?

LOOKING

VAL. That's it.

MATT. I see. So, there's no chance of anything happening?

VAL. I don't think so.

MATT. You're not interested in him that way?

VAL. Sorry.

(MATT looks at NINA.)

NINA. Sorry.

MATT. Well, you were a big help. Hygiene??

(ANDY ENTERS carrying two drinks.)

ANDY. Okay, here we go. One beer for the cop, and a Coke for the lady.

VAL. Thank you.

ANDY. So, what were you talking about while I was gone? Get me up to speed.

MATT. Oh not much. The concert.

ANDY. Right. Holly Cole. She's not going to be diving into the audience, is she?

MATT. I doubt it.

ANDY. Well, that's good news for you, Val. *(There is an awkward pause.)* So.

VAL. So.

MATT. So.

(The other three look at NINA.)

NINA. So.

ANDY. So, how's work going, Val?

VAL. Good. Good. It's quieted down now that the smallpox

scare is over.

ANDY. Oh, it's over, is it?

VAL. Yeah. They gave us the all clear on Monday.

ANDY. Well, don't cry because it's over. Smile because it happened.

VAL. What?

ANDY. I said don't cry because it's over. Smile because it happened.

VAL. It was smallpox.

ANDY. Yeah, well it's just another one of those sayings that I have. You know, like the detour one.

VAL. Uh-huh.

ANDY. And how's everything at your job, Nina?

NINA. Good. I had to take a defensive tactics recertification course yesterday.

MATT. Oh? How'd that go?

NINA. I aced it. I was poetry in motion.

ANDY. Poetry, huh? You know I read something the other day that..well, it touched me very deeply. Let me see if I can remember it.

MATT. Andy..

ANDY. 'O that 'twere possible, after long grief...

MATT. Andy, no.

ANDY. What?

MATT. I don't think they want to hear that now.

ANDY. Why not?

MATT. Believe me. They don't.

NINA. I think I've heard that before.

MATT. *(To ANDY.)* You see? They've already heard it.

ANDY. Oh. *(Pause. The he sings the first line of another well known 1960's or 1970's pop song. VAL sings the second line of the song.)* Hey, that's how it goes. You're very good.

LOOKING

VAL. I told you. Lyrics just stick with me.

ANDY. All right, try this one. *(He sings the first line of another well known 1960's or 1970's pop song. She sings the second line to the song.)* Hey, that's great.

VAL. Oh, it's nothing.

ANDY. Um...oh! *(He sings the first line of another well known 1960's or 1970's pop song. She sings the second line to the song.)* That's terrific. *(To MATT.)* You see this? Huh?

MATT. Yeah. You know what? Maybe we should head out now.

ANDY. Why?

MATT. Well, the show starts at eight.

ANDY. But, we haven't finished our drinks yet.

MATT. That's okay.

(MATT stands.)

ANDY. Well, we can stay for five more minutes, can't we?

MATT. No, we really should get going, Andy. Ladies?

ANDY. Matt, wait. Can I talk to you for a second, please?

MATT. What?

ANDY. Just for a second. Over here. Excuse us, ladies. *(ANDY and MATT move away from the table.)* What are you doing? We were starting to hit it off there.

MATT. Who was?

ANDY. Me and Val. With the song lyrics. I think I made a connection.

MATT. Andy, no...

ANDY. No, really. I think that's the magic she's looking for. Seriously. I can feel it. In another few hours, I'll be reaching over to turn her radio on.

MATT. Andy, she's not interested in you that way.

ANDY. What do you mean?

LOOKING

MATT. She's not interested.

ANDY. How do you know?

MATT. I just know. Now, let's go to the concert, all right?

ANDY. Did she say something?

MATT. No. I can just tell.

ANDY. Oh, you can, can you?

MATT. I can.

ANDY. Well, I think you're wrong.

MATT. Andy, please. It's not going to happen. Just accept it, okay? Now, let's go. *(MATT moves back to the table.)* All right, I think we're all set.

NINA. All righty.

(NINA and VAL stand.)

ANDY. Uh..Val, do you want to stay for a bit?

VAL. Stay?

MATT. Andy?

ANDY. Yeah, I mean, we can finish our drinks and catch up to these two at the concert. What do you think?

VAL. Well....

ANDY. I've got some more lyrics to try out on you. What do you say?

VAL. ......No, we should get going.

ANDY. ....Oh.

VAL. I mean, I really want to see Holly Cole.

ANDY. Sure. Absolutely.

VAL. You don't mind, do you?

ANDY. Of course not. Let's go.

MATT. All right, we're off then.

(MATT, VAL and NINA start to leave. When they realize that ANDY

hasn't moved, they stop.)

MATT. Are you coming, Andy?

ANDY. Yeah, I'll just down this beer and I'll be right behind you.

(MATT, VAL and NINA EXIT. ANDY finishes his beer and looks at the glass. He sings the first two lines to one of the songs he and VAL just sang. ANDY EXITS. A door opens and MATT and NINA ENTER. They are kissing, trying to get each other's coats off.)

MATT. Oh, God! Oh God!

NINA. Matt, wait.

MATT. What?

NINA. Wait a minute. Wait.

MATT. What's the matter?

NINA. Do you think we're going too fast?

MATT. What? Fast? What?

NINA. We're going too fast. I think we should slow down.

MATT. Oh, I like that. Good. Are you gonna give me a ticket, Officer?

(He starts to kiss her again.)

NINA. Matt, no.

MATT. Oh, come on. Gimme a ticket. And a hefty fine.

NINA. Matt, I'm serious. Stop it.

MATT. What? What's wrong?

NINA. Well, I'm having doubts.

MATT. Doubts about what?

NINA. About us. About how we got together. I mean, I slept with you on our first date.

LOOKING

MATT. And if there's any way I can repay you. Really.

NINA. It's not funny. It was our first date. Don't you think that makes me a skank?

MATT. Skank? What? Skank? Come on. Skank?

NINA. I didn't hear a 'no' in there!

MATT. No, it doesn't make you a skank. Besides, that wasn't even our date. That was Andy and Val's date. Problem solved!

NINA. But our relationship is tainted now. You'll never be able to respect me knowing that I did that.

MATT. That's ridiculous.

NINA. It's true.

MATT. Nina, I'm crazy about you.

NINA. Yeah, because I'm easy, but that'll wear off.

MATT. Wear off? It hasn't even had a chance to sink in yet.

NINA. So, you do think I'm easy.

MATT. No.

NINA. You see? It's having an effect on us already.

MATT. What effect? There's no effect.

NINA. You know what? I think you should go.

MATT. What?

NINA. I'd like you to leave.

MATT. Leave? Now?

NINA. Yes. I need some time.

MATT. Time to what?

NINA. To think. To figure out what I'm doing here.

MATT. But, Nina...

NINA. Matt, please.

MATT. I can't believe this. Everything was going so well. I mean, we met, we talked, we laughed, we made love. These are all positive things, right?

NINA. Of course they are.

MATT. And we did them in the correct order, right?

LOOKING

NINA. Yeah, in a span of two hours.

MATT. Well, now you're being unkind.

NINA. Unkind how?

MATT. Well, we spent an hour and forty-five minutes in the bar.

NINA. Look, I'm sorry, Matt, but I just don't feel very good about this right now.

MATT. About what?

NINA. About us. About me. Everything. Dammit. You know, all these years I never thought about this stuff. I went out, had fun, and if I liked the guy, well, I didn't mind sleeping with him. What's the harm, right? Now, all of a sudden I'm second guessing myself. I mean, maybe I've been wrong all this time. Shit, last month I slept with a married man. Oh, sure, I didn't know he was married, but maybe if I hadn't jumped in so quickly. Maybe if I had a more stringent screening process. Right now my screening process is 'Have you got a car?.' I mean, take you. You recite a stupid poem and boom! We're in bed. I didn't even hear the whole poem! Two lines and I'm naked. God. Why don't I take my time with these things? What's the rush? I'm living my life like it's some sort of sexual relay race and I'm the baton. That's why I don't feel so good about myself right now. Maybe it'll pass. I don't know. But at this moment I'm very angry. In fact, just looking at you makes me angry. You represent everything I don't like about myself. Every man I ever slept with and never heard back from. Every man who ever tried to hit on me with a dumb line or a silly poem. Every man I fell for because I was so damned desperate to have someone love me. You're every one of them. Standing right here in front of me. You make me sick right now!

MATT. .....So, should I call you?

NINA. I don't know. I just...I'm very confused. I'm sorry.

LOOKING

(MATT starts to leave, then stops.)

MATT. You know, all this stuff about how you feel about your-self—you'd think you'd have that sorted out by now.

NINA. What do you mean, by now?

MATT. At your age.

(MATT EXITS.)

NINA. *(To herself.)* Yeah, you'd think I would, wouldn't you?

(NINA EXITS. ANDY and VAL ENTER.)

ANDY. Thanks for the lift home, Val.

VAL. Well, when Matt drove Nina home he kind of left you high and dry.

ANDY. Right. But, you didn't have to walk me to my door.

VAL. Hey, I'm just returning the favour. Besides I wouldn't want you to get mugged.

ANDY. Naw, it's mainly old people in this neighbourhood. I can take most of them.

VAL. Have you lived here long?

ANDY. Couple of years. It was my Mom's house, and when she died I took it over. She really loved it and it didn't seem right to just let it go.

VAL. And how do you like it?

ANDY. Me? Oh, it's okay. One place is the same as the next when you live alone. I've always thought that a place doesn't become a home until it's shared with someone.

VAL. Is that another one of those sayings you have, like the detour one?

ANDY. No, that's an actual feeling. I get them once in a while.

LOOKING

VAL. I see. Well, I guess I'll get going then.

ANDY. Yeah. I'd invite you in, but the house is messy and I know how messy places embarrass you.

VAL. Right.

ANDY. You wouldn't come in anyway, would you?

VAL. ...No.

ANDY. Thought so.

VAL. So, thanks for the date. For inviting me to the concert.

ANDY. No problem. It wasn't so terrible after all.

VAL. Well, a girl couldn't ask for higher praise than that.

ANDY. No, I didn't mean the date. I meant the concert.

VAL. I know. Anyway, I'll be off now.

ANDY. Yeah. I, uh..well..

(ANDY leans in for a kiss. VAL backs off a bit but does allow him to kiss her on the cheek.)

VAL. Oh. Uh..yes... *(It is a very awkward kiss.)* Goodnight.

(VAL starts to leave.)

ANDY. Listen, have you got any tips? You know, on what I did wrong here. Just on the slim chance that I ever go out on another date. I mean, I don't want to keep making the same mistakes, you know?

VAL. Oh, Andy. There's no right or wrong. Each one of us can only be ourselves and hope that someone is attracted to our qualities. That's all it is. Just be yourself.

(VAL EXITS.)

ANDY. *(To himself.)* Be myself. That might work. If I was somebody else.

(ANDY EXITS. MATT ENTERS and sits. He is doing his radio show.)

MATT. It's eight twenty-four on Cool Jazz FM 98, and you're with Matt Kennedy. Good morning. I see where the country's largest single lottery winner just passed away. He'll be buried two feet under every year for the next three years. All right, we've got traffic and weather coming up in about five minutes. Stay tuned for that. But first, I'd like to send this next song out to a very special lady. *(ANDY ENTERS and stands behind MATT. MATT doesn't see him.)* She's not only beautiful on the outside, but on the inside as well. And somebody wants her to know that he's thinking about her, and he's hoping that she gets everything sorted out and can be happy with who she is. Because he thinks she's pretty special, and he misses her terribly, and time spent without her seems like time without end.

(We hear a song.)

ANDY. Oh, please.
MATT. Andy! What are you doing? How did you get in here?
ANDY. Walter sent me up.
MATT. Walter? Who's Walter?
ANDY. The security guard downstairs.
MATT. And he just sent you up?
ANDY. Yeah. And he wants to know if you can play some Metallica. He's dozing off down there.
MATT. So, what are you doing here?
ANDY. Oh, just on my way to the office. Gotta put out some fires today.
MATT. You got problems still?
ANDY. Yeah, you could say that. Nothing I can't handle though.

LOOKING

So, was that another request?

MATT. What?

ANDY. That 'time without end' crap.

MATT. Oh, uh..yeah.

ANDY. Same guy?

MATT. Yeah. Same guy.

ANDY. He is definitely whipped.

MATT. Yeah, look, Andy this really isn't a good time for a chat. I'm working.

ANDY. Right. So, how'd it go the other night?

MATT. How did what go?

ANDY. You and Nina. You drove her home. Did you stay over?

MATT. No.

ANDY. Uh-oh. Trouble in paradise?

MATT. No. Nothing like that. We're just taking our time that's all.

ANDY. Oh, yeah, it's trouble.

MATT. No, it's not.

ANDY. Matt, when a guy says he's taking his time it can mean only one of two things. A) The woman said no. Or B) The woman said no.

MATT. She's just going through some stuff right now, that's all.

ANDY. Yeah, who isn't?

MATT. And how did your date end?

ANDY. Oh, the usual. With a big kiss... Off.

MATT. Oh. Sorry.

ANDY. Too bad too.

MATT. Why? Do you like this woman?

ANDY. Ah, I don't know. Maybe.

MATT. Really?

ANDY. Yeah, she's nice. She's very sweet. I mean, I still think she's nuts, but..I don't know, there's something about her.

LOOKING

MATT. Well, if you really feel that way then maybe you should ask her out again.

ANDY. Hey, you're the one who said she wasn't interested in me.

MATT. Well, that's what she said.

ANDY. She said that?

MATT. In a roundabout way.

ANDY. Well, what exactly did she say?

MATT. She said she wasn't interested in you. But, hey, it's been my experience that women can change their minds pretty damned quickly. So, go ahead. Ask her out.

ANDY. Nah, I think I'll just go home tonight and stick my ass in the wood chipper. It's not as painful. So, you wanna play tennis today? Say three o'clock?

MATT. Sure. You got balls?

ANDY. *(In a ballsy voice.)* Oh yeah!

MATT. Good. I'll see you at three. Now, I've gotta get back to work.

ANDY. Sure.

(ANDY starts to leave, then stops.)

Listen, Matt, don't worry about this Nina thing. I mean, you might be feeling miserable right now, but remember this; Let no one who loves be called altogether unhappy, for even love unreturned.....aw screw it. I'll see ya'.

(ANDY EXITS. MATT EXITS. Lights up on VAL. She is in workout clothes. She's at the gym. NINA ENTERS wearing her workout clothes and carrying a magazine.)

NINA. Hi, Val.

LOOKING

VAL. Well, hi there. I haven't seen you for a couple of days. Have you been in hiding?

NINA. No, not really.

(NINA sits and starts to look through the magazine.)

VAL. And how are things?

NINA. Okay.

VAL. Just okay?

NINA. They're fine.

VAL. And what about you and Matt?

NINA. What about us?

VAL. Well, how's it going?

NINA. It's not going. It's over.

VAL. Over? Why?

NINA. Well...

VAL. Oh, no. He's married. That son of a bitch!

NINA. No, he's not married.

VAL. He's not?

NINA. No.

VAL. Then he's engaged. That son of a bitch!

NINA. He's not engaged either.

VAL. Then what is the son of a bitch?

NINA. He's nothing. He's completely unattached. Totally available.

VAL. Then why did he dump you?

NINA. He didn't dump me. It was my idea.

VAL. Your idea?

NINA. Yes.

VAL. You did the dumping?

NINA. Yes.

VAL. You?

LOOKING

NINA. Me! Is that so strange?

VAL. Well, Nina, if history has taught us anything.

NINA. Never mind! I dumped him, okay?

VAL. But I thought you liked the guy.

NINA. I do like him.

VAL. So, what's the problem?

NINA. What do you mean, what's the problem? You're the one who said I was moving too fast.

VAL. Me?

NINA. Yeah. You said I have one date and I'm falling into bed, and I dive in without checking to see what's down there.

VAL. You did this because of what I said?

NINA. Well, it made a lot of sense to me.

VAL. Nina, what do I know about men? The last time I was with a man my chest was two inches higher. God. Well, you'll just have to call him, won't you? Call him and tell him you want to try again.

NINA. I can't call him. After what I said to him?

VAL. What did you say to him?

NINA. I told him he made me sick.

VAL. You what?

NINA. It just came out.

VAL. How does 'You make me sick' just come out?

NINA. I don't know. I was on a roll.

VAL. Oh, Nina. That's terrible.

NINA. I know. It's awful.

VAL. You make me sick?

NINA. I know.

VAL. God. Matt was a good man. Had a good heart. And he really seemed to care about you. And he was attentive. I really liked that.

NINA. You know, you could have thrown those nuggets into

your 'Dive in too fast' speech. I'm gonna hit the showers.

(NINA moves to the EXIT.)

    VAL. Are you sure it's over? Is there no chance at all?

    NINA. Val, I told him he made me sick. I can't even bring myself to listen to him on the radio I feel so bad.

    VAL. Well, that's what happens when you speak before you think.

    NINA. Yeah, well that's me. Shoot first and ask questions later.

(NINA EXITS. Lights down on VAL. We hear a phone ring. ANDY ENTERS. He is carrying a small plastic storage bin. He sits in a chair. The phone continues to ring.)

    ANDY. I'm not here! *(The phone continues to ring.)* Give it up. I ain't answering. *(The phone stops ringing.)* Thank you. Persistent bastards.

(VAL ENTERS. She is still wearing her workout clothes. ANDY doesn't see her. He sings the first line of another well known 1960's or 1970's pop song. She sings the second line of the song.)

    ANDY. Val.

    VAL. Hi.

    ANDY. What are you doing here?

    VAL. Well, I tried calling your cell but it wasn't on.

    ANDY. Yeah, it finally gave up the ghost.

    VAL. And then I called the office number here but there was no answer.

    ANDY. Oh, yeah. Well, I had to let my receptionist go. And I haven't been answering it myself because it's probably just creditors.

VAL. Oh? Something wrong?

ANDY. Wrong? Well, how can I put this? Uh...the business folded.

VAL. Oh, no. I'm sorry to hear that.

ANDY. Well, it happens.

VAL. Andy, that's terrible. What are you going to do?

ANDY. Oh, I'll be okay. I've got some money socked away. I'll be fine.

VAL. Well, that's a relief.

ANDY. Yeah, I'm good until Thursday. So, now I'm just packing up a few things and getting the hell out.

VAL. Andy, I'm really sorry.

ANDY. Nah, it's okay. Hey, life's a rollercoaster ride, right? All you can do is hang on and scream. So, if you've come for some storage space, well, I'm afraid I can't help you.

VAL. No, that's not why I'm here.

ANDY. You're sweating.

VAL. I just came from the gym.

ANDY. You didn't shower?

VAL. I was in a hurry to get over here.

ANDY. Looks like you didn't even towel off.

VAL. I was in a hurry.

ANDY. Why? What's up?

VAL. Well, I don't know if it's a good time now. I'm mean, you're out of business. You're probably depressed. You must feel like a total failure.

ANDY. ...Actually, I hadn't thought about that. So, what can I do for you, Val? What do you need?

VAL. Well....you have to ask me out again.

ANDY. Excuse me?

VAL. You have to ask me out. On a date.

LOOKING

ANDY. Really?

VAL. Yes.

ANDY. Tell me something. Does this mental illness run in your family?

VAL. Andy, I'm serious.

ANDY. So am I.

VAL. No, you see Nina broke it off with Matt because of something I said and now she's sorry about it but she thinks he hates her and he probably has a good reason to because of what she said to him so you have to ask me out again and then you have to tell Matt to ask Nina out because I said I don't want to go out with you alone.

ANDY. All right, I'll ask you again.

VAL. Good.

ANDY. Does this mental illness run in your family?

VAL. Andy, please. I know we didn't really hit it off and I know you probably don't ever want to see me again, but just this one last time for Nina and Matt. Please.

ANDY. You're serious.

VAL. Completely.

ANDY. She's serious. All right, what the hell? Val, would you like to go out with me again?

VAL. I'd love to.

ANDY. Will you shower first?

VAL. Definitely.

ANDY. Where am I taking you?

VAL. To a play.

ANDY. Aw jeez. First a jazz singer and now a play. When is it?

VAL. Tomorrow night.

ANDY. And how am I going to pay for it?

VAL. I'll pay for it.

ANDY. No, I've got too much pride for that.

VAL. Forget your pride.

LOOKING

ANDY. Done.

VAL. Now just get Matt to call Nina and we'll meet you at the bar at six-thirty.

ANDY. Meet us? No listen, if I ask you out I would definitely offer to pick you up?

VAL. No no, we'll take the bus. That way Nina won't have a ride home after the play and Matt will offer to drive her.

ANDY. And how do you know she'll accept?

VAL. Oh, any girl would rather get a ride than take the bus late at night. A guy would have to be pretty insufferable for us to choose otherwise.

ANDY. Oh. So I assume I'll be driving you home?

VAL. No, I'll take the bus. So, you'll do this then?

ANDY. Yeah. Sure.

VAL. Oh, thanks Andy. Thank you so much. I know this is asking a lot.

ANDY. Hey, no problem. You're just lucky I like you.

VAL. Yeah. What?

ANDY. I said you're lucky I like you.

VAL. Oh.

ANDY. What's wrong?

VAL. Nothing. Nothing. Well, I guess I'll be going then.

ANDY. Yeah.

VAL. And I'm really sorry about your business.

ANDY. Thanks.

VAL. You like me?

ANDY. Yeah.

VAL. But why? I mean, I've been so cool and detached on our dates.

ANDY. Yeah, well, that's how I like my women. In fact, if you start ignoring me completely, you'll never get rid of me.

VAL. Oh, I see. You're joking.

ANDY. Right.
VAL. Oh. Good.

(VAL turns to leave.)

ANDY. But not about liking you.

(VAL hesitates for a moment and then EXITS. ANDY picks up the container and EXITS. MATT ENTERS with his cell phone. NINA ENTERS with her cell phone.)

MATT. So anyway I guess he decided to ask her out one more time and she said yes but she said she didn't want it to be just her and Andy for some reason. I mean, she's been out with the guy twice already. She can't go out with him alone yet? Tell me something. Is Val nuts?
NINA. Yes she is.
MATT. Well, that explains it then. So Andy asked me to ask you to go so that we can be the buffers but if you don't want to go it doesn't matter. Doesn't matter one bit.
NINA. ...Yeah, I'll go.
MATT. You will?
NINA. Sure.
MATT. Really?
NINA. Sure, why not?
MATT. Oh, okay. Its tomorrow night.
NINA. Fine.
MATT. And Andy said that if you said yes then Val said you two will take the bus in and meet us at the Dick.
NINA. Why did she say that?
MATT. Because she's nuts I guess.
NINA. All right. I'll see you tomorrow night then.

MATT. Now, you're sure about this, huh? Because I don't want you to feel that you have to go just because Val's your friend.

NINA. No, I'll go.

MATT. You're sure?

NINA. Yeah.

MATT. All right.

NINA. What about you? Do you want to go or are you just asking me because Andy's your friend?

MATT. No, it doesn't matter to me one way or the other.

NINA. Doesn't matter to me either.

MATT. Good. As long as we both couldn't care less, let's do it. *(NINA EXITS. ANDY ENTERS and sits at the table. MATT moves to the table and joins ANDY. We are at The Private Dick. It is the night of the play.)* So, you can start on Monday then?

ANDY. Yeah, sure.

MATT. Great. I'll tell them.

ANDY. And all I have to do is...

MATT. Make sure nobody gets up to the radio station without being authorized.

ANDY. Sounds easy enough. I feel kind of bad for Walter though. I feel like I was partially responsible for him getting fired. Ironic, isn't it?

MATT. Yeah. So, here you are, huh? Another date.

ANDY. Yeah.

MATT. And she agreed. I told you women can be fickle. So, she said yes right away huh?

ANDY. Immediately.

MATT. Hmm. But why a play? Since when are you interested in the theatre?

ANDY. Hey, I've been to the theatre.

MATT. What for? To use their washroom?

ANDY. No, I saw some one man show once.

LOOKING

MATT. How was it?

ANDY. Not worth it. Forty bucks to see one person? If I'm payin' forty bucks, I want to see a gang fight up there.

MATT. How much did you pay for tonight's tickets?

ANDY. Enough.

MATT. God, you must really like this woman if you're willing to spend money you don't even have on her.

ANDY. I suppose.

MATT. Well, let me tell you something, Andy. It's her loss if she doesn't feel the same way. You're a helluva guy. A woman would be lucky to have you.

ANDY. Well, that's very nice of you, Matt.

MATT. I'm just sayin'.

MATT. And what about you and Nina? What's happening there?

MATT. Well, she sounded pretty disinterested on the phone. I think she's just coming tonight for Val's sake.

ANDY. Maybe you should tell her how you feel.

MATT. I told her how I felt. I told her I was crazy about her.

ANDY. And what did she say?

MATT. She said I made her sick and she threw me out.

ANDY. So it didn't go well.

MATT. No. So, I'm not saying a word tonight. If she's got something to say to me then fine, she can do the talking. I'm all talked out.

ANDY. And of course they're late again. Look at that. Six forty-five. *(He tries to flag down a waitress.)* Waitress? Excuse me?! No, that's fine. Just keep going. I'm invisible. Have a nice night, you self-indulgent harpy.

MATT. I'm gonna go to the bar and get a drink. Are you coming?

ANDY. Are you buying?

MATT. Yes.

LOOKING

ANDY. Then I'm coming.

(ANDY and MATT EXIT. VAL and NINA ENTER. NINA waves to someone off stage.)

NINA. Hi Tony!

VAL. Who's Tony?

NINA. The hunk in the white t-shirt.

VAL. Oooh he is a hunk. How do you know him?

NINA. I arrested him last year. Indecent exposure.

VAL. Oh.

NINA. So, why are we going to a play? Andy doesn't seem like the kind of guy who enjoys the theatre.

VAL. Oh, no. He told me he enjoys it very much.

NINA. Uh-huh. I still don't know why you said yes. I mean, you gave the guy two tries and you said there was no magic.

VAL. Well, you never know. Maybe I missed something. Besides, I really want to see this play.

NINA. What's it called?

VAL. Rasputin. It's a one man show.

NINA. So, where are they? Do you see them anywhere?

VAL. Uh...yeah. They're at the bar.

NINA. They're always at the bar. Just once I'd like them to be waiting for us when we arrived.

VAL. Let's sit.

(VAL and NINA sit.)

VAL. So, are you nervous?

NINA. Yes. I mean, God Val, I told him he makes me sick.

VAL. Well, he seems like the forgiving kind. And you did say he was one of the few good ones out there. It would be a shame to let him get away.

NINA. Well, it's not like I haven't let men get away before. The only ones I seem to be able to hang onto are the ones I put in handcuffs.

VAL. In the line of duty you mean.

NINA. ....Yeah. God, you know, things are supposed to change when you get older. You're supposed to learn from your experiences. This relationship thing should be easier now, shouldn't it?

VAL. No. Every relationship is different. You start a new one, everything you've learned goes out the window and you start fresh.

NINA. Well, that bites ass.

VAL. Look, maybe he's forgotten about the whole 'you make me sick' incident.

NINA. Would you forget about something like that?

VAL. Not a chance.

NINA. Of course not. And what about me? What do I say to him? Am I supposed to pretend it didn't happen? Do I just smile and say 'Hi, how are you?'

(MATT and ANDY ENTER.)

ANDY. Hi there.

NINA. *(Smiling.)* Hi, how are you?

ANDY. Glad to see you finally made it.

VAL. Sorry we're late. I'm not familiar with bus schedules. I don't ride them very often.

MATT. You know, we could have picked you up. You didn't have to ride the bus.

VAL. Oh, well, I never thought of that.

MATT. You mean Andy didn't offer?

VAL. Uh...Well...

ANDY. No, I didn't. I'm sorry. I was just so thrilled that you said yes, I guess I lost my head.

VAL. Well, we're here now. That's the main thing. Right?

ANDY. Yes indeed. It sure is. *(MATT looks at NINA.)* Well, as long as you're up, Matt, how about getting the ladies a drink?

VAL. Oh, do we have time? How much time do we have?

ANDY. Oh, we've got a few minutes. Time for a quick one. What'll it be?

VAL. All right, well, let's see. What do I feel like? Uh..maybe a Caesar. Yes. How about you, Nina?

NINA. I'll have a beer please.

(MATT is staring at NINA.)

VAL. All right, one beer and one Bloody Caesar.

(MATT doesn't move.)

ANDY. Matt? Did you get that? A beer and a Caesar. *(MATT still stares at NINA.)* Matt?

MATT. I've got something to say to you, Nina.Now, I tried saying it the other night and you told me I made you sick but I'm going to give it another shot anyway because I just don't know when to quit. I'm like Andy here. Like some idiot who's willing to keep trying even though it's futile. Even though his heart is going to get stomped into the ground. Even though..

ANDY. Okay, point taken.

MATT. And who knows, maybe I didn't say it right the first time. Maybe my inflection was all wrong. Although I am a broadcaster by trade and it is my job to communicate so I doubt if that was it. Maybe you just weren't listening. Maybe in your haste to get rid of me and wallow in self doubt, you didn't hear what I said. So here it is again. And listen closely because I'm only going to say this twenty or thirty more times. Nina, I'm crazy about you. I am. And I'm telling you right here in front of everybody in this bar. I don't care who hears it!

ANDY. Nobody's listening.

MATT. I don't care! Did you hear me that time, Nina? I'm crazy about you. And I don't want this to end before we've given it a real solid try. And if you still want some time, then that's fine. If you want to go slow, we'll go as slow as you want. I'm in no rush because I happen to think you're worth the wait, so I'll wait. I'll wait as long as it takes. Because I think we're good together. No, hell, I think we're great together. And I can't live without you. All right, that's a bit much. Of course I could live without you. What am I gonna do? Die? No. I'll go on living, meet somebody else, settle down with her, and that'll be that. But I would much rather be with you than her! So, that's it. That's what I wanted to say. I'm crazy about you Nina, and if you don't give me a chance to be the love of your life then the rest of my life will seem like a drive down a dark and endless road.

VAL. Oh, that is beautiful.

MATT. *(To VAL.)* And you! What's your problem? This is a sweet guy. Give him a chance for God's sake! What the hell is wrong with you women!? *(To NINA.)* So, what do you say, Nina? Do I still make you sick, or do you want to smarten the hell up and give this thing a try? Or do you want me to tell you again? Huh? Because I will if you force me to.

(NINA stands.)

NINA. You have the right to remain silent.

(NINA kisses MATT. A long kiss that makes ANDY and VAL somewhat uncomfortable. After the kiss, NINA takes MATT's

hand and they EXIT.)

ANDY. ......So that was a Caesar, right?

VAL. Yeah.

ANDY. *(Andy stands.)* Right. Well, I'll get that for you, and then we can head out.

VAL. Or maybe we should just head out now. I mean, the theatre's four blocks away. We should probably just go.

ANDY. Oh. Okay. Or maybe you'd rather just go home. I mean, the Matt and Nina problem appears to be taken care of.

VAL. Yes, it certainly does.

ANDY. And that's why we're here, right?

VAL. Right. Do you think they'll make it to the play?

ANDY. I don't think they'll make it to the car. So, maybe you'd just rather go home.

VAL. Well...

ANDY. Yeah, you'd rather go home. That's fine.

VAL. No. I mean, I've got the theatre tickets anyway. We might as well use them.

ANDY. Oh. Okay.

VAL. Unless you'd rather not.

ANDY. No, that's fine. I'll go. What the hell.

VAL. Good. Well, that's what we'll do then.

(VAL stands.)

ANDY. What's the play called by the way?

VAL. Rasputin.

ANDY. Ooh, the mad monk. Bolsheviks. Oughta be a couple of big fight scenes in that one.

(ANDY and VAL EXIT. ANDY and VAL ENTER again. It is

about three hours later. ANDY is walking VAL to her door.)

VAL. Well, thanks for the ride home, Andy.

ANDY. Oh, no problem. It was better than taking the bus, right?

VAL. Yes it was.

ANDY. Good. And thanks for the play.

VAL. Did you like it?

ANDY. Well, I had no idea Rasputin was such a talkative fellow. Three hours. Wow. I thought he'd never shut up.

VAL. So, you didn't like it.

ANDY. Not really.

VAL. Well, at least you're honest.

ANDY. Well, there's no need to lie to try and impress you now, right? I mean, there's nothing happening here, so I can just be myself like you said.

VAL. You think you have to lie to impress me?

ANDY. Oh, yeah.

VAL. Why?

ANDY. Well, there's not much to me, so I have to lie to bring myself up to your level.

VAL. My level?

ANDY. Yeah. I mean, a woman like you? What would you want with a guy like me? Hell, I can't even keep a business running. And it's not like it was a challenge, right? Selling storage space? How hard can that be? Too hard for me apparently. I've got a new job though. Yeah. I'm a security guard. I start Monday. I'll be trying to stop demented jazz fans from rushing the studio and lighting mood candles. Yeah, I'm pretty pleased about that. That's a real step up for me. So, this? You and me? I knew I didn't stand a chance the first time I laid eyes on you. You're too good to be true so how could it work? But, I gave it a shot anyway. You gotta give me credit for that. You know, that first night, I was hoping you might invite me in

LOOKING

to talk—Seriously. Just to talk. That's all I wanted to do, because you seemed like someone who was easy to talk to, and maybe I could have made a case for myself—But, that didn't happen and I can see why. I mean, when a woman invites you in, it usually means there's at least a chance that sex will ensue right? And I can see why you wouldn't want to lead me in that direction, because that particular event is very special. You know what the most exciting part about making love to a woman is? For me, I mean? It's the fact that the woman would actually allow me to do it with her. And I'm not selling myself short here, don't get me wrong. I mean, I can hold up my end in the lovemaking department. No, I'm in there plugging all the way. But, to think that a woman would want to share something that intimate—that personal—with me...well, that thought excites me and satisfies me and fills my heart all at once, because that is such a wonderful gift. So, uh.. *(He looks at his watch.)* Oh, boy. Look at the time. I've been rambling on like Rasputin. I'd better let you go. So, I guess this is goodnight then. And, uh..well.. *(Andy leans in and gives Val a kiss on the cheek.)* It's been nice knowing you, Val. It's been very nice.

(ANDY turns to leave.)

VAL. Andy? Would you like to come in?
ANDY. Come in?
VAL. Yeah.
ANDY. You want to talk?
VAL. .....We could.

(VAL holds out her hand. ANDY takes her hand and VAL kisses him on the lips. Lights down. End.)

LOOKING

PROPERTIES PLOT

Two tennis racquets
Two gym bags
Four towels
Hand weights
Newspaper
Beer in glasses
Four cell phones
Red clown nose
Concert tickets
Business card
A list of adages
Napkin
Magazine
Storage bin
Telephone
Files
Papers

LOOKING

COSTUMES
ACT ONE

Tennis scene
Both Andy and Matt are in tennis shorts and tennis shirts and tennis shoes

Gym Scene
Both Val and Nina are wearing workout outfits

First bar scene
Andy - Sport coat, dress shirt, dress pants, casual shoes
Matt - Dress pants, loose fitting dress shirt over a t-shirt, casual shoes
Val - Dress, high heels
Nina - Dressy jacket over a blouse and jeans

Radio Station scene
Matt - Casual shirt, jeans, casual shoes
Andy - Long trench coat over dress shirt, dress pants and casual shoes

Second gym scene
Val - Workout clothes
Nina - Sweater, jeans and casual shoes

Phone scene
Matt - Casual shirt, jeans, casual shoes
Nina - Sweater, jeans and casual shoes
Val - Coat over workout clothes
Andy - Long trench coat over dress shirt, dress pants and casual shoes

LOOKING

ACT TWO

Second bar scene
Andy - Sport coat over shirt with slacks and casual shoes
Matt - Sport coat over shirt with slacks and casual shoes
Val - Pant suit, heels
Nina - Skirt, blouse, heels

Second radio station scene
Matt - Casual shirt and pants with casual shoes
Andy - Long trench coat over dress shirt, dress pants and casual shoes

Third gym scene
Val - Workout clothes
Nina - Jeans, sweater, shoes

Andy's office scene
Andy - Shirt with sleeves rolled up, loosened tie, slacks, casual shoes
Val - A coat over her workout clothes

Second phone scene
Matt - Casual shirt and pants with casual shoes
Nina - Jeans, sweater, shoes

Third bar scene
Andy - Sport coat, dress shirt, dress pants and casual shoes
Matt - Sport coat, casual shirt and pants with casual shoes
Val - Casual jacket over tank top and slacks, heels
Nina - Casual jacket over sweater, jeans and shoes